A SCHOOL OF RED HERRINGS

Who killed the groom? The murderer must have stood in line to wait his turn...

JANICE EDWARDS—a widow before she was a wife. Had she found out about the parade of women in her bridegroom's life?

GRACE NICHOLS—the marriage-minded mother who refused to take "no" for an answer. How could she let Janice escape the embrace of her favorite son?

LOU NICHOLS—The intended . . . by all but Janice.

THOMAS NICHOLS—the jealous brother, always watching. He was determined to save Janice from all but himself.

GAMALIEL FITZGERALD—impoverished publisher, he hired a poor mouse and watched her blossom into an elegant heiress. Was Janice too rich for his blood . . . or too necessary for his future?

Also by Rae Foley,
 Soon to Come from Jove/HBJ

PUT OUT THE LIGHT
WHERE HELEN LIES
SUFFER A WITCH
THE BROWNSTONE HOUSE

ONE O'CLOCK AT THE GOTHAM

Rae Foley

A JOVE/HBJ BOOK

Copyright © 1974 by Rae Foley
Published by arrangement with Dodd, Mead & Company

All rights reserved. No part of this publication may be reproduced or transmitted in any form or by any means, electronic or mechanical, including photocopy, recording, or any information storage and retrieval system, without permission in writing from the publisher.

First Jove/HBJ edition published March 1978

Library of Congress Catalog Card Number: 73-17863

Printed in the United States of America

Jove/HBJ books are published by Jove Publications, Inc.
(Harcourt Brace Jovanovich)
757 Third Avenue, New York, N.Y. 10017

*For the Authors' League of America
and Rex Stout in Homage*

ONE

IN A HEAVY fog Carl Ransome crashed his plane into the side of a mountain and was killed instantly. His wife survived for a day without regaining consciousness. When all the legal tangles had been cleared away, Janice Edwards learned that, as her mother's sole heir in a will drawn up before her second marriage, she had inherited the estate of her stepfather, which consisted of holdings in a wide range of prosperous enterprises, and his pet project, Inspiration Lake—the name was his—with a considerable acreage of forest land as well as the lake itself, which made it the largest private holding in the Adirondacks.

Successful as he had been as a businessman, Carl Ransome had regarded himself as a frustrated artist, having had a vague desire as a boy to become a sculptor. Though he had made no push to do anything about this tentative ambition, he felt that he was more spiritually akin to creative people than to the members of his own group, a conviction which misled no one and gave him a great deal of satisfaction.

Inspiration Lake was to compensate for what he sincerely believed to be his own deprivation, a refuge for people working in the arts, a flourishing colony to surpass anything yet established in the country.

He started his project by building an ornate inn, which

he named Leisure Land, with a golf course, tennis courts, and the sports afforded by the lake: swimming, fishing, boating, water-skiing. There was also a good dance band for weekends, an excellent bar, and a cellar stocked with fine wines to do justice to the *cordon bleu* cooking.

The inn was ostensibly designed to provide relaxation for the members of the colony and amusement for any guests the artists might care to entertain which the cottages were too small to accommodate. It afforded a place where Ransome could entertain financiers of his acquaintance and a group of wealthy sportsmen whom he frequented. With his customary acumen he charged off this hospitality to business expenses and the rates for guests were so excessively high that the inn showed a profit on his investment within a remarkably short time, for there are always people to whom the mere ability to pay exorbitant prices is a simple pleasure in itself.

The next building to be constructed was Peaceful Haven, an enormous, sprawling, rustic lodge, which Ransome occupied during the summer months with his second wife and occasionally, but as rarely as possible, with his stepdaughter. The house was ably managed by John and Mary Bertie, a couple whose sense of obligation for a small loan, repaid long since, was so great that their combined salaries cost Ransome less than he would have had to pay for a daily cleaning woman.

No one, as his friends agreed, could invest money more intelligently. When Ransome cast his bread upon the waters, it came back toasted and spread with caviar—the best caviar. He could and did get his name on countless lists of benefactors and sponsors of various worthy causes without being a penny the worse for it.

The one part of his ambitious program to lag was provision for indigent artists. Only six cottages had been built, and of these only three had ever been occupied.

Ransome's first wife had brought him a comfortable nest egg and after a dozen years of mutual boredom she had died quietly, without causing him any trouble or leaving him with awkward encumbrances in the shape of a family.

It was typical Ransome luck that he should encounter the beautiful widow, Dorothea Edwards, at a gala performance to which some kind friends had taken her, as Dorothea's late husband had left her too ill-provided for to attend such gatherings on her own.

At once they had recognized their compatibility. At thirty Mrs. Edwards was at the peak of her stunning beauty; she had a charm of manner that was irresistible and that would, Ransome recognized, make her an outstanding hostess. For her part, the opportunity to move out of the half-world of genteel poverty into the limelight as Carl Ransome's wife might almost be termed the equivalent of love at first sight.

There was only one drawback to this felicitous union: Mrs. Ransome's daughter by her first marriage. To a woman who had been hailed as a beauty from the time she was a toddler, it was a constant humiliation to have to acknowledge as her own child a tall, gawky girl with braces on her teeth, who had no charm and, besides, looked her full age, which was an affront in itself.

Ransome had accepted this burden without complaint, and had dealt with the matter with his usual kind firmness. When he realized that nothing could be done to make Janice attractive and interesting to his friends, he felt no obligation to keep her with them. As calmly as he would have removed from his walls a painting whose authenticity was doubtful, he placed Janice in a succession of schools and summer camps until she was really too old to be kept there any longer.

As Janice was as reluctant to go into society as her mother was to have her, it occurred to her stepfather to determine whether she had any ideas of her own.

"So far as I can make out," he told her, tapping a pencil on the polished desk in his library, "you have no particular interests."

"Or abilities," she agreed.

"No, no, I didn't say that. But if you had just been interested in any of the arts—"

"I'm interested in all of them. I'm the one who listens

to the music and looks at the paintings and reads the books." There was the glint of a smile in her eyes—large hazel eyes fringed with dark curling lashes, her one beauty. "Without people like me the creative ones would have no one to admire them."

Ransome did not care for flippancy, and in a young woman of no discernible attractions, flippancy was out of place. "You can't, after all, spend the rest of your life reading novels."

"Why not?" she asked unexpectedly. "It's what I really like." It was, she reflected, the way she lived her real life.

"Trash," he said scornfully. "Women's fiction. *Cinderella*. Mere entertainment."

"What's so mere about entertainment? It makes life a lot more bearable. And it's not just a woman's escape. What do men like to read? A so-called adult version of an oversexed *Jack the Giant Killer*."

Ransome sighed and later reported to his wife that he had had a talk with Janice and it had not been satisfactory —not at all satisfactory.

She sighed, too. "You've always been so wonderful to her, Carl! There is nothing you have begrudged her. I can't understand how she can be so ungrateful, so uncooperative."

"I suppose this means," he said in resignation, "that we'll be dragging her around with us wherever we go from now on."

As it happened, this desperate situation never arose. A few days later Janice announced that she had found a job.

"A job? But what can you do?" Ransome demanded.

"I'm going to be a kind of girl Friday to Gamaliel Fitzgerald, who has bought over a small publishing house."

"A small publishing house! Another fly-by-night outfit without sufficient capital. It's not," he demanded in horror, "one of those outlets for adult books?"

Janice laughed. "Not at all. It's perfectly respectable."

"I hope," her mother said plaintively, "you'll be careful to explain that this extraordinary idea is quite your own and Carl is not responsible for it. He's never refused you anything."

In spite of past experience Janice had hoped, faintly, but still hoped, that her mother would be interested in her plans, which was, of course, unreasonable of her.

"My boss doesn't know I have any connection with the great Carl Ransome."

"Janice!" Her mother's tone was sharp. "That was gross impertinence."

"Sorry."

"I suppose this means you'll have no time for the Guilder charity matinée. I was counting on you to make lists and call people and take care of the arrangements."

"No time at all," Janice agreed cheerfully, and she went out of the room with her usual slouching walk, an attempt to compensate for her height.

Her mother looked after her and sighed. "Poor Janice! Sometimes I wonder what will become of her, as helpless as she is. And yet it would not do for her to have any considerable amount of money. She's a born victim, if I ever saw one, and a single kind word would make her fall for the most impossible man."

She got up to look at herself in the long mirror, skin still smooth and glowing from the constant care it received; dark eyes that had not faded; glistening black hair that was discreetly touched up and showed no gray. She had worn well, she thought complacently, very well. No one would think she was the mother of a twenty-three-year-old daughter, certainly not that she was Janice's mother. In the mirror she saw her husband's eyes rest approvingly on her and she blew him a kiss.

II

The advertisement in the HELP WANTED—FEMALE section of the paper had caught Janice's eyes after she had looked despondently at appeals for bookkeepers, stenographers, machine operators, kitchen workers, and salesgirls, for none of which positions she had any aptitude. So it was with delight that she read the ad:

WANTED by small publisher. Girl Friday to handle fiction and miscellaneous jobs. Salary minimal. Work maximal.

Gamaliel Fitzgerald, Publisher, had two small rooms on a court in a Fifth Avenue building. Seeing the sign, WALK IN, Janice did so. Even to her inexperienced eyes it was obvious at first glance that this was, indeed, a small company, apparently a one-man outfit. There was a long counter cluttered with unopened mail and manuscripts and beyond it a desk with a typewriter and a telephone.

In a second room, opening on the dark court, a long bony sort of man with a large nose prominent in a thin face sat with his fingers clutching at his hair, absorbed in a manuscript.

That was Janice's first view of Gamaliel Fitzgerald. When he did not notice her, she knocked lightly on the counter, and when this brought no response, she said tentatively, "Hem."

He called impatiently, without looking up, "Well? What do you want?"

This wasn't promising. Anyhow, you can't apply for a job and appear at your best by yelling across two rooms, so Janice lifted the hinged counter and went in.

"I came to apply for the job."

"Good God! You don't mean it." He got to his feet, even taller and narrower than she had realized, unfolding like a jackknife, and stretching out a long arm to pull up a chair for her, brushing some papers onto the floor. "Sit down, Miss—"

"Edwards. Janice Edwards." She sat down with the light on her face, studying him gravely while he summed her up.

"So you want to work for a publishing house. Why?"

She considered the matter. "Well, when I looked at the ads, there was nothing I was really qualified to do—"

He chuckled. "So obviously you figured you could fit in here."

"Not exactly, but I like to read—"

"I tried to suggest," he said in measured tones, "in that unfortunate advertisement of mine that there would be other tasks. Reading is fine, but you need more than that. Do you know what makes a book sell? All right, you don't need to answer that. No one knows. You'd have to answer the telephone and pay the bills and take care of the mail and, in the unlikely event that one of these scripts is worth publishing—because newcomers like me, with little financial backing, get only what's left in the bottom of the barrel—you'd have to read copy and correct proof and—"

Janice sighed and got up. "Sorry I took up your time."

Unexpectedly he grinned at her, a boyish grin that stripped years from his age. "You can see perfectly well that I have all the time in the world. I didn't say you couldn't have the job. Good God! You're the only one foolish enough to apply for it."

At that Janice began to laugh, spontaneous laughter that bubbled up, transforming her face. Then quickly she pressed her lips together. The publisher sat back for a double take. Too tall, awkward, almost ungainly, shy, rather plain except for her lovely eyes. Then she laughed and she was really something. A stunner. Drab brown hair worn long and hanging limply, which merely emphasized the length of her face. A retiring church mouse—until she laughed. He looked at her with the stirring of a Pygmalion.

"But why," he began again, "a job in publishing?"

"Well, after all, I have to do something."

He noticed the handmade shoes, the sable jacket she had tossed negligently over the back of a chair, the beautifully cut suit she wore so badly. One thing was sure: she didn't need a job to provide her with three meals a day.

"Why don't you travel?"

"I'm not adventurous." She was surprised and a little amused at the way this unorthodox interview was going.

"Why don't you go into society?"

"I'm too shy."

"What about a life devoted to good works?"

"Charity is no real answer to human ills."

"And have you," he asked her politely, "found the real answer to human ills?"

To her horror Janice found herself making a face at him.

He scowled. "Why don't you learn the arts of homemaking? That's a nice womanly career for a girl."

"It would be wasted. I'll never marry. And I don't think they want me to hang around the house. Why should they? Look at me, for heaven's sake."

He did so, taking his time. "Well," he conceded handsomely, "you've got your problems," and Janice found herself holding back her laughter with difficulty. "You know what you need, girl? Take dancing lessons and learn to kick up your heels."

"Have you ever seen a maypole dancing?"

"No lip from you," he said, warming to his task. "This is advice from the horse's mouth. Learn to walk as though you were twelve feet tall, and proud of it. Walk as though you were accustomed to breakfasting off the tops of trees. Did you ever see a giraffe with stooped shoulders?" He answered his own question. "No self-respecting giraffe. And put your hair up instead of letting it hang like that. Then you can attract attention to your eyes. They're terrific, but they get lost in the general disaster area." As she rocked with laughter, he added gravely, "There's no charge for this advice."

"I don't know why you should feel called upon to give me advice. What I'm looking for is a job."

"All in good time. Choosing a girl Friday is no simple task, let me tell you. You never know what you might be letting yourself in for."

"And why," she astonished herself by asking, "did you advertise for a girl Friday? So far as I can make out, it's a slavey you have in mind."

He acknowledged this palpable hit. "Sounds better the other way, though."

"And what influenced you in choosing this thriving business?" She glanced at the piled-up manuscripts, the unopened mail, the general disorder.

"That's a sad story. I had only a little capital so it seemed best to pick up a small business on its last legs." He looked around and shook his head. "It still is."

"What would you have preferred to do?"

"I wanted to be an explorer until I fell off an Alp and broke a shoulder. I thought anthropology would be my meat but I learned I had no taste for primitive living and upset my digestion for a year by eating native food. So—behold me. What I'm doing here I can't imagine. You don't get rich and you don't get famous. You gamble money you can't afford on a book and then no one pays any attention to it or it gets a two-inch notice in the back of *The New York Times Book Review* and ends up on the remainder table in drugstores, a fate worse than death. The printer earns more money than most writers and the publisher goes broke or sells out to a big corporation diversifying its interests—and its risks. It's a mug's game and you'd be smart to stay out of it."

"Then why are you in it?" she asked, entertained.

"Because," and for once he was serious, "it's the one place that still has complete freedom of the press and it will continue to have it as long as the Authors' League flourishes. If I had a fortune, that's where I would leave it and be sure of doing some good."

"Whether by accident or design, you've landed in the place that's right for you. You really love it."

"Flattery," he told her severely, "will get you nowhere. Are you sure you want a job here? I can't pay more than a hundred a week. If you can type—"

"Oh, I can do that."

"Well, we'll have a go at the mail and you can enter those scripts on the card file and sort them into categories: nonfiction, specialized books, juveniles, fiction: straight, romantic, historical, suspense, Gothics—and the latter, incidentally, you can read for me. A woman's viewpoint on woman's fare."

Her eyes glinted with indignation and he watched sympathetically while she struggled with her temper. "Okay, suppose we get down to work and tackle the mail first."

"Before we do anything else, I'm going out to buy a duster and clean up this place."

"Who's the boss around here?" he asked, and returned to his script.

From that first meeting Janice and Fitz had quarreled, bickering happily all day long, and she had never laughed so much in her life. She also began to transform herself. She followed his advice about dancing lessons. She wore her hair up and she wore her clothes with more distinction as she acquired a good carriage.

Every day they went around the corner to the Gotham for lunch, sometimes alone, more often with an author or an agent. Within a matter of weeks Janice's friends learned that she was never available for lunch because of that inflexible appointment at the Gotham.

"Why," Fitz demanded one day, when she had stopped laughing abruptly and pressed her lips together, "don't you ever let yourself go? You no sooner smile or laugh than you tighten your mouth as though it were a trap."

"I suppose it's because as a child I had to wear braces and they looked so awful that I was ashamed and tried to cover them."

"You might look at yourself when you are laughing. Nothing there to stop a clock or give a horse colic. I've seen worse. Not often, of course, but still worse."

Janice's laughter broke off when the outer door opened and the man who was to do jacket designs appeared. She returned to her desk and a script from the pile marked Gothics.

TWO

SIX MONTHS after the fatal plane crash in the Vermont mountains, the senior partner of the law firm of Perkins and Scott awaited with considerable interest the coming of Janice Edwards. He had known Ransome well; he had been acquainted with the charming Mrs. Ransome; but the girl who entered the office, escorted by the junior partner, was unexpected. She was tall, her hair brushed smoothly around her head and folded into a thick knot in back. She walked proudly, carrying her height well, but, except for her lovely eyes, she had no trace of her mother's stunning beauty.

The junior partner had long since attempted to explain to Janice that she was the sole heir to the estate of Carl Ransome when the large estate would finally be settled.

Her response had taken him by surprise. "There must be some mistake."

He had relayed this unexpected reaction to the senior partner who now explained patiently that Ransome had left his entire estate to his wife, who survived him by one day, and that her will, drawn up before her second marriage, left everything to her daughter, who, therefore, inherited both estates.

Janice listened gravely but without evidencing any sign of gratification. "Well, perhaps you are right. That is, there seems to be no error on your part. This is what Mr. Scott told me some months ago. But the whole thing is a mistake. A dreadful mistake. My stepfather never for a moment intended me to have all that money; neither did my mother, for that matter. She didn't think I would know how to handle it, and anyhow, she didn't really like me, you know."

She brushed aside impatiently the flustered and shocked protests of the two lawyers. "Let's not be hypocritical about this. My mother was always ashamed of me. If she had known that she was going to die she would never, never, have left me all that money!" There was an unmistakable ring of conviction in her voice.

The senior partner was the first to recover his poise. "However that may be, Miss Edwards, the fact remains that as soon as we can settle the estate, and these things take time, the property will be legally yours. You will want to decide what is to be done with it but you must not rush into anything impulsively. There is a good deal of responsibility attached to that kind of estate. My own suggestion would be that you make no changes until you have had time to give the whole matter some consideration and have consulted your own lawyer, if you would prefer not to leave matters in our hands. My advice would be to leave your investments unchanged; they are diversified enough for safety and as secure as anything can be in today's market."

He glanced at notes on his desk. "Then there's the question of that property your stepfather bought on Inspiration Lake." He grimaced as he pronounced the name. "There's an exceptionally fine inn and so much land around the lake that any shrewd developer could create an exclusive summer colony at an enormous profit. Enormous. Of course, if you had more business experience, you might prefer to develop it yourself, but for that, of course, you would need expert advice. There are pitfalls for the inexperienced, the unwary." He shook his head. "Pitfalls."

"No," Janice said, "that's out. My stepfather intended to create an art colony at the lake for workers in the fields of music, painting, and writing. I'd like to carry out that plan to the best of my ability. That would mean putting up a number of cottages, perhaps gradually extending them back into the woods, but widely enough scattered to ensure complete privacy, and without, of course, altering the character of the place, clean air and clean water and wildlife protected."

"That's a big project for an untrained girl and it would involve drawing heavily on capital instead of adding to it. Mr. Ransome never operated in that way." Perkins added dryly, "As you know, he built only six cottages for his art colony and never filled more than three of them, one of the occupants being Vladimir Strunski who can hardly be said to need free lodging as he is one of the most distinguished composers alive today."

"But, like all composers, he requires privacy and quiet in which to work. In any case, there is no need for further discussion. I have made up my mind to develop the art colony. Why, even if the place weren't reserved for working artists it would be important to keep it in character. The country needs more than housing. It needs areas of open space and trees and wild life and a place of peace."

For a diffident young woman she could really dig her heels in, the younger partner thought. He smiled at her in a way that generally won the confidence of women clients, though it did not seem to make much impression on this one. "I cannot agree with your decision, Miss Edwards, but I respect your motive. This is designed, I gather, as a kind of memorial to Mr. Ransome."

To his surprise she laughed, transforming her face. Almost before he was aware of the change she said, "I never liked him any better than he liked me. But this," she added outrageously, "is the only decent and generous thing he ever proposed in his life and I'd like to make it work. So far the colony has never been more than a token but I want to turn it into a reality. Perhaps that money is going to be good for something, after all."

She looked at her watch. "I'm flying up to the lake this afternoon for the first time in months. I've never been back since the accident. There will be a lot to attend to there as well as here in New York. Something will have to be done about the town house. I've moved into an apartment and I'd like to dispose of the house. Perhaps you will handle that for me." Her brisk manner took them aback. This girl seemed to have no difficulty in making up her mind.

"What about the furniture?"

"It might be sold at auction, I suppose. Some of the stuff is valuable and," she added dryly, "all of it is expensive. None of it was ever mine. I always felt like a stranger there. An unwelcome stranger." She was not bitter; she seemed to take a detached view of her plight. "A friend let me have her apartment rent-free when she went abroad and I think I'll buy it." She smiled and again her face was alight and radiant. "I believe I am going to enjoy having money of my own to spend." She pushed back her chair and stood up. "The chartered plane for the inn leaves at five o'clock. I really can't give you any more time now."

"There's just one thing, Miss Edwards," Perkins said so urgently that she resumed her seat. "You're a very well-to-do young woman now. You should not remain intestate for a single day. The tragic and unforeseen deaths of Mr. and Mrs. Ransome illustrate how uncertain life can be. If you will give me your instructions—"

"I'll have to think about it. This is all new to me." But she was thinking. "I suppose the best thing would be to set up some sort of foundation to finance the colony at Inspiration Lake. I can see that, with steadily rising costs, a great deal of money will be required to clear the land, build the cottages and maintain them."

The senior partner made notes. "How about personal bequests?"

"I have no family, no—" Again she smiled and this time the two men were waiting for it. The transformation was as profound as the change from tragic to comic mask in a Marcel Marceau pantomime. "Oh, yes, I'd like to leave a hundred thousand dollars to Gamaliel Fitzgerald to help him maintain his publishing house."

"Fitzgerald?"

"He's my boss and heaven knows he could use the money and put it to good account, if anyone could."

"That's a considerable amount to leave to a comparative stranger." As Janice arched her brows in aloof inquiry, the protest died. Perkins cleared his throat. "We'll have a draft of the will for your approval sometime next week and at that time we'll be able to go into the matter in depth." He shook hands with her, smiling, but when the junior partner returned from escorting her to the elevator, the smile faded. "I hope she won't confide to this Fitzgerald that she has left him all that money."

Scott shook his head. "He must be a very persuasive guy. A sitting duck. That's what she is. A sitting duck."

II

The pilot, who had been waiting impatiently for Janice to arrive, lost no time in getting airborne. She looked around the chartered plane, which on Tuesdays and Fridays took residents at the lake for a day's shopping in New York. On Friday it also picked up weekend guests for the inn, returning them Sunday evening.

There were only a few faces she recognized, among them a prominent television actor who was probably a guest of the Strunskis. Most of the passengers were prosperous businessmen who flew up to spend weekends with wives and families who summered at the inn. The only one she knew well was Hal Streichen, who came to sit beside her, saying predictably, "Long time no see."

As there was no need to reply to such a comment, Janice did not bother.

He shook his head sadly. "It must be tough on you, coming up here all alone. How long has it been?" His voice was suitably hushed.

"Since they were killed? Almost six months." Her matter-of-fact tone discouraged sympathy.

Hal gave her a veiled glance which she did not observe.

She had never paid much attention to him, though he had his uses when she was prevailed upon to make one of her infrequent and reluctant appearances at the inn, as he could be counted upon to ask her to dance.

Meanwhile he was studying her covertly. A long drink of water, too tall for his taste. He liked to look down on women literally as well as figuratively. She had none of her mother's good looks. Even at forty-five Dorothea Ransome had been something to look at. Poor Janice had nothing but those gorgeous eyes. Still there was something different about her. She had come swinging along to the plane without her usual slouch, holding her head high. There was even a kind of grace about her movements and she wore her clothes better. A new hair-do gave her face a piquant quality and, for once, she was wearing earrings that brought out the color of her eyes.

Of course, he reflected cynically, with the Ransome money it wouldn't matter much how she looked. It wouldn't matter at all. Why, the property at the lake alone would be a nice plum, a mouth-watering plum.

"I heard you'd be coming up this afternoon. Back to stay?"

"No, just for the weekend. There are a lot of things to straighten out with Mrs. Bertie and I want to look over the whole place. I'm going to carry out Mr. Ransome's original idea and make this a really useful art colony, a place where, I hope, some significant work can be done."

"Mr. Ransome. You always called him that, didn't you?"

"He would probably have exploded if I had called him Carl, and I can't say he ever yearned to have me address him as Father."

He laughed uneasily. In the past Janice had not been so outspoken. Coming into the money must have given her self-confidence. Coming into that much money would give anyone self-confidence. Prickly sort of girl, he had always thought, and he'd been careful to keep out of her way except for doing the polite to please Ransome, but now the situation was changed. She was definitely worth a little trouble.

"Say," he exclaimed, "I was so pleased to see you that I forgot my guest. Let me introduce him, will you?" Without waiting for her consent, he stood up and beckoned. "Janice, this is Bob Maxwell, an old friend who's making his first visit to the inn, but not, I hope, his last. We've got to make him like the place. He deserves it, you know. He's a POW just released and he ought to have a red carpet laid out for him. Bob, this is Janice Edwards."

Janice, looking up at Hal's guest, was surprised to find him so unlike his willowy friend. Maxwell, at thirty-five, had a big frame, dark hair with traces of white at the temples, a pleasant face with rather blunt features, and level eyes that held hers when he took her hand in a firm grasp. He had a nice voice, too.

"Don't pay any attention to Hal," he begged her.

"No one does," she assured him, and at Hal's suggestion took the middle seat with a man on either side of her.

"How did things go at the colony during the winter?" she asked Hal.

"About the same. The status is always quo. Peters is still painting pictures that no one buys. Mrs. Nichols—and why does she rate living rent-free in that cottage now that her husband is dead? He was the only creative one in the family, if you call a writer who never got published creative."

"Just before he committed suicide, her younger son was drafted, so Mr. Ransome let her stay on."

"She has Thomas to look after her."

"Yes, but since Lou was reported missing in action, Mrs. Nichols has spent every cent she could dredge up in an attempt to find him."

"That's ridiculous."

"Of course it is, and horribly unfair to Thomas, but as long as she clings to the hope that Lou is alive somewhere, she'll be all right. If she ever admits to herself that she's unlikely to see him again, I think she'd crack wide open."

"Thomas," Hal explained to his friend Maxwell, "is the worthy son, a natural beast of burden. He carries two jobs in order to support his mother and give her the extra money she demands. He is patient with her. He lets her have her own way about everything—and what happens?"

"She wipes her feet on him," Maxwell suggested.

"I wonder how often," Hal said, "she makes clear to poor old Thomas that she resents the fact he is alive and her darling is gone."

Janice turned to find that Maxwell was smiling at her and she instinctively smiled back. He blinked in surprise.

"Hal ought to warn you, Mr. Maxwell—"

"Bob," he suggested.

"If Mrs. Nichols hears there is a POW at the inn, she'll try to see you and find out whether you were in the same company as Lou and if you ever heard of him. She'll haunt you."

"She'll drive you nuts," Hal said, grinning.

"For God's sake, Hal, cut out this returning war-hero stuff, will you? Let's forget it if we can."

"Sure, sure," Hal agreed amiably. "You know," he said to Janice, "I was just remembering how Mr. Ransome made capital out of the news that Lou was missing. His public relations man wrote a tear-jerker about the missing war hero and how comfortably his grieving mother was housed at the expense of Carl Ransome, philanthropist and art patron. Art patron! And all that on the basis of one writer who took poison because he hadn't made good and one painter who will never make good. Nice going for such a small outlay."

Hal Streichen was under thirty, a young-old man with thinning hair, lines of dissipation on his face, and bloodshot eyes. He was rarely completely drunk, rarely completely sober. A harmless creature if one did not mind his waspish tongue; good-humored unless he was expected to do something he had no desire to do and that might put him to some trouble. He toiled not. It was generally assumed that he had an adequate income from his family, as he was able to pay the exorbitant rates of the inn for a suite of rooms which he maintained all year round. He dressed well and he had excellent manners. Now and then he exerted himself to be attentive to young women or not so young women who came to the inn unescorted and presumably able to afford its charges. But whether his constant state of mild inebriation drove them away or whether he could not decide to commit himself, he was still unmarried.

"You may be right," Janice acknowledged, "that, so far, this is a phony art colony, but you forget Vladimir Strunski. Not even you can say that Strunski is not a great musician."

"Even I!" Hal protested, and again she disconcerted him by making no comment. "Okay, so Strunski is great, but I can see why Ransome wanted to have him here. His presence gives the place prestige and he can collect around him some of the most famous and interesting people in the country. What I can't figure out is why the Strunskis are willing to stay on where there is none of the kind of life they are used to: the cosmopolitanism, the sophistication, the glamour and excitement."

"Vladimir Strunski likes the quiet. He can't compose in an uproar. Living in that small cottage, he and Sonia have to do their entertaining at the inn, which means that he can regulate the number of people he sees and the time when he sees them. He wrote that D minor piano concerto up here and the tone poem and a contata that will have its première in the fall. When Sonia doesn't like the quiet of the cottage, she can find plenty of gaiety at the inn."

"You don't like Sonia?" Hal asked idly.

She looked at him in surprise. "Of course I do. She's charming and different from other women, like something out of *The Merry Widow*."

"You've lost me," he admitted.

"I know what she means," Bob Maxwell put in. "Old Vienna and Strauss waltzes and hand-kissing and trailing skirts and hats with sweeping plumes. The crystallization of feminine glamour. A woman whose every gesture and expression carries the most delicate implication of sex."

"That's it exactly."

Hal looked from one to the other. "Well," he drawled, "you two seem to be *en rapport*. The beginning of a beautiful friendship."

Janice ignored this, but Bob was annoyed. "Hal says there is dancing at the inn on Friday and Saturday nights. I hope you'll come."

After dreading these sessions for years, as only a wallflower can dread them, Janice was surprised to find how much she wanted to go. In the first place, she wanted to display how well she had learned to dance; in the second place, she found that she wanted very much to dance with Bob.

"Not this weekend, I'm afraid," she said reluctantly. "I have a tremendous number of things to attend to."

He took her hand as they prepared to land. "But you'll be back another time? Oh, that wouldn't do me any good."

"Sure, sure," Hal said. "Delighted to have you. Come as often as you wish. You can get in some water-skiing."

"That would be fine. In the meantime, Miss Edwards, may I call you in New York?"

"Of course." She gave him the phone number at her apartment. "But you can't reach me there during the day. You'll have to call me at the office."

"Office!" Hal ejaculated.

"I'm a working girl. Gamaliel Fitzgerald, Publishing. You can reach me there, nine to five, except between one and two, when we always lunch at the Gotham."

"We?" Hal inquired.

"Fitz and I. And usually, of course, an author or an agent."

"Oho! Bob, you'd better get cracking if you want to make time with Janice before she's snatched up."

There was a glint of anger in Bob's eyes as he looked at Hal, who was being deliberately mischievous, but he smiled at Janice. "See you soon, I hope." He went with Hal toward the waiting limousine that had come to collect the weekend guests for the inn.

She looked after him, the smile still lingering on her lips.

THREE

RANSOME'S HOUSEMAN, looking older and more shrunken than she had remembered, put her suitcases into the back of the station wagon, but Janice insisted on sitting in front with him.

"I want to hear all the news. How are you and Mrs. Bertie?"

"My wife's been busy all week cooking for you. She says there is no satisfaction in getting meals for me because I eat so little." Bertie put the car in gear. "We were mighty sorry to hear about Mr. and Mrs. Ransome, as we wrote you. Mighty sorry."

Considering that her stepfather had left nothing to the couple who had served him at an inadequate wage for nearly fifteen years, Janice wondered why. At least she was now in a position to make up to them for what Ransome had failed to do. She explained mendaciously that he had left both Bertie and his wife pensions which would enable them to live in reasonable comfort.

For a moment she was afraid that he was going to cry. His Adam's apple bobbed up and down in his scrawny throat in an alarming manner. At last he said, "Then you'll be bringing up some servants of your own."

"Not unless you would rather retire. I'd be delighted to

have you stay on, but what with rising living costs we'd have to arrange a more realistic salary, don't you think?"

"Miss Edwards—" After a struggle the old man gave up and drove on in silence.

As the red disk of the sun dropped, night closed in on them, and the narrow road, carved through the heavy forest, was a dark tunnel pierced by the headlights. Janice was glad that she had remembered, in the stifling heat of New York, to bring a topcoat, and she slipped her bare arms into it, grateful for its comforting warmth.

And now the road opened and the lake lay before them, shimmering softly, the red faded to an opaline hue. This was the narrow neck of the lake on which the inn stood, a blaze of lights. Then, as the road curved, there was only the glitter of water on the great lake. Spaced at wide intervals, there were three rustic cottages which had never been occupied, for Ransome had abandoned his temporary dream of an art colony, or at least it had served its immediate purpose of affording him a great deal of publicity as a sponsor of the arts for a minimum outlay.

Something must be done, Janice thought. So many struggling artists would enjoy this peace, the privacy afforded by the woods, the financial relief of living rent-free—people who might otherwise have to abandon their creative work in the struggle to support themselves. Suitable candidates must be found whose creative abilities could be vouched for by authorities in their respective fields, for otherwise the whole project would be meaningless. Perhaps Vladimir Strunski would know of someone, or she might ask Fitz. It was typical of her whole relationship with her boss that she had never mentioned the Ransomes or the art colony at Inspiration Lake.

The Peters cottage was dark, which didn't mean that they were away. They never went away. Probably they were sitting on their screened porch, looking out at the dark lake, speaking or silent but always in some sort of close communion. If she could choose the kind of marriage she wanted, Janice would unhesitatingly take the one that most resembled the relationship that Jake and Helen Peters had created.

The next cottage had outside lights burning, which meant that the Strunskis had gone to the inn to welcome their weekend guests and dine. Later they would dance. At least Sonia would dance. Strunski declared that, at seventy, he was too old for gymnastics, but he enjoyed watching his wife. At any rate, that is what he said.

A light burned in the kitchen of the Nichols cottage where Mrs. Nichols was preparing dinner for Thomas. She would probably serve him spaghetti, which he disliked, because it was cheaper than meat and every cent must be spent on the search for Lou. Janice shivered, and Bertie, mistaking the gesture, switched on heat in the car. There was something terrifying, chilling, in that mother's grim obsession with her missing son, her determination that he must be found and found alive, her unalterable conviction that he and Janice had been engaged to be married and only his being sent to Vietnam had prevented their marriage, or rather postponed it.

Before the weekend was over, she would inevitably come to see Janice to discuss plans for the wedding that was to take place when Lou returned, which was the chief reason why Janice had put off for so long her return to the lake, though, of course, the thing had to be faced sooner or later.

In a way, she thought, as Bertie pulled up at the big, rambling rustic lodge with its weather-beaten shingle reading PEACEFUL HAVEN, everyone at the lake knew what everyone else was doing at any given time, knew everything there was to know about each other—everything except what mattered.

When she had been greeted warmly by Mrs. Bertie and regaled with an enormous meal, Janice stretched out on a long chair on the screened porch. Here there was neither sight nor sound of the inn. Around the great curve of the lake the music of the band could not carry. There was only the lapping of water whipped by the breeze against the dock and soft, furtive sounds from the woods, which were alive with small creatures and, of course, larger ones: deer and cougars.

Tomorrow, Janice thought drowsily, she would have to perform the duties she had already gone through in the New York house, sort out her mother's possessions and dispose of them.

Sooner or later, she would sell Peaceful Haven, which was too big for a woman alone; and she had never been happy here, an intruder on sufferance. But tonight she felt its enchantment and its peace, almost a welcome, which was illusory, as she knew.

Tonight she would put all the problems out of her mind. Tonight she was going to rest and dream and listen to the soothing, rhythmical lapping of water against the dock, and then tumble into bed for a long sleep with so cold a breeze that she would need a blanket. Perhaps two blankets.

She found herself thinking about Bob Maxwell, who was an unexpected sort of friend for Hal Streichen to have, a pleasant man with pleasant ways. And he had liked her as much as she had liked him. She wondered if he was dancing at the inn. Sonia Strunski would lose no time in having Hal present his personable guest. She was always on the lookout for suitable partners. As the forty-year-old wife of a seventy-year-old husband she was constantly looking for escorts. This situation the aging composer appeared to take in his stride, though there were times when a gleam in his eyes indicated that he was not as reconciled as he claimed to be.

It would be fun to be at the inn, dancing with Bob, displaying how much she had profited by her dancing lessons, and wearing a new dress. And then Janice chuckled at herself and the dazzling picture of her in Bob's arms, the cynosure of all eyes, the envy of all the women, a desirable object to all the men. Anyone would think she was fifteen and not too bright at that. Nonetheless, she hoped that Mrs. Nichols would not learn that Bob was a POW and pester him with questions about her missing son and the war he so obviously wished to forget, which would give him a dislike of the inn. At any rate, he had said he would call her in New York. It was something to look forward to.

And then the telephone rang. The Berties, tongue-tied, red-eyed, but smiling, had gone to their room, doubtless to talk of their great good fortune and bless their benefactor, Carl Ransome, who for fifteen years had exploited them in the kindest possible way.

The voice at the other end of the wire was unmistakable—soft, musical, with a faint foreign accent. Sonia Strunski had lived in so many countries and spoken so many languages that there was none which she did not speak with an accent now, even her native Russian. As a rule there was a kind of languor in her speech, as there was in her voluptuous movements, not distinct but implicit. Tonight she was breathless.

"Janice? Oh, good. This is Sonia and I am in a tearing hurry. We're dining at the inn with some friends of Vladimir, a young baritone who wants to sing for him—he's after a part in the contata Vladimir is preparing for fall—and a TV actor who is a real charmer for looks but so dull! How few men can combine physical attractiveness and brains. I do love creative men. That's why I've been faithful to Vladimir."

As Janice laughed outright, she said in total unconcern, "Well, in my fashion, of course. Anyhow, that's not the point. My God, how I do wander! Look, Janice, I understand that Inspiration Lake belongs to you now. Vladimir has an idea that he would like to buy his cottage and stay on here all year round. No and no and no! Never. Stuck here for months at a time, except when he is a guest conductor somewhere or attending rehearsals or having a première. Impossible! He has a fixed idea that he works better here, which is absurd. He worked just as well when we lived in France or Switzerland or Italy. Even in New York, for that matter. So if you love me, please be adamant. Tell him that you refuse to sell. But don't, for God's sake, tell him I called you."

"Don't worry, Sonia. I don't intend to sell anything here at the lake except, possibly, Peaceful Haven, and I won't do that this year. In fact, I am going to turn this into the kind of colony it always should have been."

"How assured you sound, darling," Sonia said in surprise. "Having money must be good for you. Well, I suppose it is good for anyone. 'Bye now. See you tomorrow. Cocktails at the inn at five-thirty."

Janice was on her way back to the porch when the telephone rang again. This time it was Helen Peters. "Janice, how are you, my dear? I hate to think of you rattling around all alone in that big house, and on your first night, too. I couldn't ask you to dinner because Jake is on one of his working jags and quite insupportable. I'm thinking of taking an ax to the man. Anyhow, what about lunch tomorrow? Just the two of us, if it doesn't bore you to talk to an old woman. Probably a scratch meal, as I haven't had time to shop, but I know you won't mind. A little spartan fare will make Mrs. Bertie's cooking taste all the better."

"Look here, why don't I bring a casserole? Mrs. Bertie has prepared enough food for a regiment."

Janice could hear the smile in Helen Peters's voice. The older woman was quite aware that Janice was providing food to supplement an inadequate larder. "That will be fine! Twelve-thirty all right? Though, of course, it won't matter as long as you are bringing your own food." The smile was gone now and though she attempted to speak lightly, there was a strain in her voice. "I suppose you are preparing to sell out. You won't want to be bothered by the lake and the inn and the cottages and all that."

Knowing the intolerable anxiety Mrs. Peters must be under in case her husband should be dispossessed from the cottage that had sheltered him for years, Janice said quickly, "Oh, I'm not going to sell. I'm planning to create an honest-to-God colony here. I can't wait to tell you all about it and ask Jake's advice."

There was a long-expelled breath and then Helen Peters said, "Oh, there's one thing. If you'd like me to sort out your mother's clothes, just say the word. It's a painful job; I had to do it for my mother and it's so much easier for an outsider, don't you think?"

Jake and Helen Peters were regarded as a helpless couple—vague, disorganized, impractical. But it was always they who were aware of one's most pressing need and tried to find a solution.

The third call came just as Janice was starting upstairs to bed. Her heart sank when she recognized the flat, monotonous, plaintive voice of Grace Nichols.

"I've been waiting all evening for you to call me. Well, Janice, it's high time you came back, though I must say you might have let me know. Who has a better right? Not a word from you all these months except in answer to my letter of sympathy. And what with the fighting men out of Vietnam and the POWs coming home. Lou may be here any day and we've got to make some plans. For instance, I can't decide whether it would be better for him to live at Peaceful Haven, at least until he gets adjusted to civilian life, or whether he'd rather be in your New York town house where there's more going on."

As Janice was speechless, Mrs. Nichols went on. "I can't say that I'd care much for New York, now that I'm used to the quiet up here, but, of course, it would be easier for Thomas and save him this weekend commuting, which runs into money, I can tell you. And sometimes I wonder why he bothers to come because he hardly talks to me any more. Tonight I started telling him about you being back and all the planning there is to be done for when Lou comes home and he just walked out. And where he could go in the dark on foot, I'm sure I don't know. Well, why I called you—and I wouldn't even have known you were coming if I hadn't just happened to meet Mrs. Bertie the other day when she was putting in supplies—a leg of lamb with prices what they are! But I suppose that won't matter to you now—well, as I was saying, I just called to tell you to come to dinner tomorrow. Six o'clock. Probably a cheese soufflé, so don't be late. Standing ruins a soufflé."

It wasn't an invitation; it was an order. And what, Janice wondered blankly, did the woman expect? Did she think that if Lou returned, which was unlikely, and if Janice married him, which was improbable, that the entire Nichols family was to be housed in one of the Ransome establishments? The woman's obsession was getting close to the brink of madness.

Janice went to test the lock on the door, forgetting that this was a precaution people at the lake rarely used. She heard the creaking sound of oarlocks and the thud of feet as someone jumped on the dock. She switched on outside lights and saw the thick-set man who came up the path toward her with unhurried steps.

"Well, Janice, I began to be afraid you were never coming back. It was only tonight Mother said she'd heard that you'd be here for the weekend and she wants you to come to dinner tomorrow."

"She told me so," Janice said dryly. "Sit down, Thomas."

He had heavy features, hair that grew low on his forehead, making a thick brush, and a sober, deliberate manner that made him appear much older than his thirty years. It was as hard to imagine Thomas young as it was to picture what Lou might have become in middle age. Lou, laughing and feckless and carefree. Lou with his exasperating and sometimes painful practical jokes and his curious indifference to the trouble he caused. But likable in a way that Thomas, good, dependable, worthy, was not. Which was unfair.

"Mother's already called you? I suppose you know what she wants." Even when Janice had seated herself on the long chair, Thomas stood hovering uncertainly.

"Yes, of course; she wants me to marry Lou."

"That's why I came. Lou has had everything all his life. Everything he wanted. But not you, Janice. I think if you were to marry him, I'd kill him!"

II

"You're shivering," Thomas said solicitously. "We'd better go inside. Or at least let me bring you a wrap of some sort."

Janice recovered her voice. "For heaven's sake, Thomas!"

"We can't talk until you are warm and comfortable."

"We aren't going to talk at all tonight. If we've got to talk, we can do it tomorrow when I go to your cottage for dinner."

Thomas stood balancing himself against the back of a chair. "If we've got to talk!" He laughed shortly. "I can imagine just how much of a chance I'll have to talk to you at home. I had to sneak out tonight and come by boat in order to see you without Mother finding out and raising hell. She's got you earmarked for Lou and she'd never stand for you marrying me. And she'll never, never accept the fact that he is dead. So if we're going to have any happiness, we've got to take it without consulting her."

"But, Thomas," Janice began helplessly, feeling like an inadequate swimmer who has got into a strong undertow.

"Come inside where you'll be warm," he insisted. "Please. inadequate swimmer who has got into a strong under tow. you only knew—"

A kind of underlying despair in his voice made her yield, however reluctantly, and she led the way into the rustic living room with trophies of Ransome's killing on the walls. There were big couches, a number of comfortable lounge chairs, tables and lamps. Bearskin rugs were spread on polished floorboards.

Janice had never cared for the place on which Ransome's insistent virility had stamped itself. At least Bertie, with his usual thoughtfulness, had laid a fire of birch logs and she bent over to thrust a Cape Cod lighter under them and drop in a match. She stood watching the fire catch, run around the end of a log, burst into bright and cheerful flames, instinctively postponing the moment when she would have to listen to her first proposal of marriage.

Then Thomas thrust her gently down onto a couch facing the fire. It was the first time she had ever been aware of his touching her, and something about the soft, padded fingers pressing her bare arms gave her a feeling of revulsion.

"Do sit down, Thomas! Don't stand there hovering. It's unnerving. But only for an hour." You can stand a dentist's drill for an hour if you have to, she reminded herself.

"I suppose I should be grateful for small blessings." His voice was bitter.

"Are you trying to pretend that you are in love with me?"

He flushed darkly. "There's no pretense about it. I've been in love with you for two years, but I was hamstrung because Mother insisted that you were engaged to Lou and she'd have hit the roof. What with her anxiety about him, I just couldn't do anything to make matters worse for her."

"Listen to me, Thomas," Janice said in a tone of exasperation. "I was never engaged to Lou. That's an idea your mother got in her head after he was reported missing, and I couldn't shake it. I've tried and tried, but she doesn't listen to me. I never dreamed of marrying Lou. I was never in love with him. If he came back tomorrow, it wouldn't make the slightest difference. Is that clear?"

"Thank God for that! I hoped it was that way. Lou wasn't your sort. But what with the report that he was missing in action, and Mother convinced that you belong to him, I've been in a hell of a spot. I couldn't make a move. I couldn't say anything. I couldn't make a push to get you. But tonight I had it up to here, so I decided to see you and speak for myself. I always knew Lou would be wrong for you. He was a playboy and he would never have grown up. If he had lived to be seventy, he would still have thought it was a good joke to pull a chair out from under a cripple. And you remember those tear-gas sprays he used to carry around and all the trouble they caused? And he was no kid; he must have been over twenty at the time."

Janice made no reply. This was an aspect of Thomas she had never suspected—a passionate, bitter Thomas. A potentially violent Thomas.

When the silence had lasted for some time, he said, "I'd do anything in the world for you. Every time you look at me with those wonderful eyes, my heart turns over. No man could love you more devotedly than I do." He turned away to stare at the fire, to kick back a coal that had shot out on the rug. "I guess I make a pretty dreary appearance. The guy who is at his mother's beck and call. Such a good son! You know why I had to take the rowboat out tonight? Because Mother would raise the roof if I drove Lou's car except to have it serviced and kept in good shape for him. It's a relief that my vacation ends on Monday and I can go back to work in New York, heat or no heat." He turned around, forcing himself to meet her eyes. "I suppose I don't seem like much of a man, but I don't think I could bear to have you come to the cottage tomorrow and discuss marrying Lou. There's a limit to what a man can take."

"Thomas," Janice said gently, "let me repeat what I said. In no conceivable circumstance would I marry Lou and, honestly, I don't know how this maggot got in your mother's mind. I can't remember that he ever liked me especially. He liked girls who were little and fluffy."

"He liked all girls. What he didn't like was having to work for his living. Mother knew that. And she knew, of course, that sooner or later you would come into the Ransome money."

"But I never expected to get it! What's more, Mr. Ransome never expected me to get it."

"That may be true, but Ransome had no children of his own, no brothers or sisters, no one but your mother. It stood to reason that the estate would be yours eventually." There was no sound in the room but the crackling of the fire. At last Thomas said humbly, "You wouldn't consider me, would you?"

"I'm sorry."

"Okay. No reason why you should, of course."

Something in his misery hurt her. "Let me fix some

drinks. There should be quite a supply in the buffet. Mr. Ransome always kept it well stocked."

"Thanks. Not tonight." Thomas spoke with an effort. "I'll be on my way. See you tomorrow." Unexpectedly he jerked her up from the couch and into his arms, plastering her face with rough, inept kisses. Then he released her so abruptly that she staggered. "Well, at least I've had that much. Good night."

Janice heard the door slam, heard his footsteps on the dock, heard the scrape of oarlocks as he pushed off.

Poor Thomas, she thought. Poor Thomas. And then she wiped her face carefully with her handkerchief, trying to scrub away those distasteful kisses.

FOUR

NEXT MORNING, with the assistance of Mrs. Bertie, Janice went through the clothes and personal belongings her mother had kept at the lodge, smelling the familiar scent of the sachets in the filmy underwear, remembering how her mother had looked in the various dresses, wondering, as she had so many times before, who was more to blame for the estrangement between them.

How very unlovable I must be, Janice thought, and then recalled Thomas's profession of love the night before, again with a shiver of distaste. He had surprised her both by his rough kisses and by an unexpected vein of violence.

When the clothes had been sorted she gave the sweaters, two fur coats, and several sports outfits to Mrs. Bertie, who promptly burst into tears. "It's too much. It's just too much. The nicest things I've ever had."

Second-hand clothes, Janice thought. How little Mrs. Bertie had ever had. How little most people had. She had, unexpectedly, been given so much, yet it was she who was dissatisfied, expecting something more. Happiness, perhaps.

Later, a grateful Mrs. Bertie, with many cautions about burning herself, gave her a large casserole of turkey mornay, still bubbling, and wrapped in towels, which Janice balanced carefully on her lap in the station wagon.

"I'll walk back," she told Bertie.

The Peters cottage, like all the others, had a screened porch running the length of the house, a large living room with a fireplace, two bedrooms and a bath, and a compact kitchen with a dining area. At the back and adjoining the cottage, so it would be unnecessary to go out of doors in bad weather, was a studio.

Helen Peters opened the door before Janice had carried the casserole up the two shallow steps that led to the porch.

"Careful! It's scalding hot. Just out of the oven."

"Good heavens," Helen exclaimed as she saw the size of the casserole. "Enough here to feed the whole colony."

"You know Mrs. Bertie. She's always thwarted because she doesn't have scads of people who appreciate her cooking."

"We'll have sherry and then eat at once while it is still hot. I do wish Jake could be lured from work to have some of this. I don't think the infuriating man has eaten a solid meal since he started painting in such a frenzy."

Helen Peters was sixty, slender, almost scrawny, with thinning white hair, wearing jeans and a rough shirt, moccasins on narrow feet. Her eyes had faded and so had her complexion, and there were fine lines creasing her lips.

On the wall, dominating the living room, was a fulllength portrait of her as a young woman, for which Peters had received many offers and which, even when almost penniless, he had refused to sell. She was wearing a Spanish costume, her black hair held up by a high, ornate comb, a vivid shawl over her shoulders, one hand on her hip, head tilted in a laughing, challenging manner. Alive, vivid, lovely, young.

Over small glasses of excellent sherry—Jake did not object to economizing on food, but he refused to do so on wine—Helen chatted lightly about life at Inspiration Lake. On the whole it had been an eventless winter, with fewer guests at the inn than usual, except for the weeks of winter sports.

"But I thought Mr. Strunski always managed to attract interesting people up here?"

Helen smiled. "My dear, it isn't Vladimir, it is Sonia

who attracts them. She has a talent for gathering creative people around her, not because she is a celebrity hunter, and not so much because they are men, though there is that, of course. The thing is that Sonia has a rare gift; she can stimulate creative impulses in others though she is not creative herself. You remember Falstaff being the cause that wit is in other men. I've seen it time after time. What a pity she feels she has to prove she is irresistible when her real strength lies in her talent for fertilizing the creative minds of others."

Helen's contribution to the lunch was French bread she had just baked and a tossed salad. It was not until they had done justice to the casserole—"There's plenty to heat up for Jake's supper"—that Helen asked casually, "Have you heard from Mrs. Nichols?"

Janice groaned. "I'm going to have dinner there tonight."

"I thought she wouldn't waste any time asking you."

"She didn't ask me; she told me to come."

"Oh, dear! But you can't help feeling sorry for the poor thing. It must be terrible not to know whether your son is dead or alive."

"She has two sons."

"I know. We tend to overlook Thomas, don't we? Such a good son. So devoted."

"Personally," a voice grated from the doorway, "it is my conviction that Thomas hates his mother's guts. Someday, and you may quote me, he is going to smash like Humpty Dumpty."

Helen laughed. "Trust my dear husband to look at the sunny side. Do sit down and have some of this delectable dish Mrs. Bertie made."

Jake Peters, a little shorter and stouter than his wife, with a rough thatch of white hair and rugged features, pulled out a chair and seated himself.

"For heaven's sake, Jake, where are your manners?"

He grinned amiably at Janice and rose to make a formal bow. "Miss Edwards, this is an unexpected pleasure." He dropped back onto his chair, reaching with paint-stained fingers for the plate his wife was passing him. Then he turned to Janice. "Is this hail and farewell or are you back permanently?" His manner was always casual; he was incapable of pretense, but there was no one with whom Janice felt more at home, perhaps because he accepted her as naturally as she did him, in spite of the difference in generations.

"Neither one." She outlined her plan for increasing the scope of the colony. While he ate his lunch, he nodded from time to time, but she was not misled. His mind was still on the canvas he had left in the studio. She accused him of it.

"May I see it or would you rather not?"

"Come along," he said with alacrity, pushing back his chair. "There's a lot still to be done, but I've said all the essential things. The basic statement is there."

As usual his studio smelled of turpentine and there were filthy rags on the floor. He brushed one off a stool for Janice. The easel had been placed near the window to catch the north light, a long narrow canvas that was almost stark. There was a glimmer of water, dark and brooding under a night sky. There was a suggestion of distant woods, a silver light that might be reflected moonlight snared in the water. The woods seemed to be infinite miles away.

Janice looked at it for a long time. "I think it's the best thing you have ever done. It's what you've been groping for, isn't it?"

He was gratified, but he said, "At sixty? It's too late, of course."

"Nothing of the sort. Verdi changed his style and composed his greatest opera at eighty. Dickens couldn't have written *Our Mutual Friend* in the days when he produced *Oliver Twist*. He didn't know enough; he wasn't mature enough. Why, this is what you were meant to do. Isn't it, Helen?"

"I think it is splendid," Helen agreed.

"Oh, Helen always builds up her old man."

"Helen does nothing of the sort," his wife retorted. "I didn't like your last two paintings at all."

"Jake," Janice said, "will you let me buy this when you've finished it?"

He pretended to stagger. "My God, we've got a paying customer. Take care of her, Helen." As there were footsteps outside, he muttered, "Oh, God! Sonia the siren in person. Let's go back to the house. I don't want her in the studio. She'll never be satisfied until I paint her."

They trooped into the cottage and Helen opened the door for Sonia Strunski, who was, as always, a completely finished work of art. Her hair was an expert dye job, a marvelous bronze shade. Her eyelids were blue and false lashes added depth to them. Her face was delicately made-up. A sleeveless blue dress with a matching sweater slung over her shoulders molded her plump figure. She wore a heavy scent. She had, Janice remembered, the kind of skin that seems to absorb perfume so that the scent never entirely dissipates.

She nodded to Jake and Helen and came to press a fragrant cheek against Janice's and say, "My dear, we are so glad to have you back. We've missed you. I know you're having cocktails with us this afternoon, but I couldn't resist seeing you first, all by ourselves. Mrs. Bertie said you were lunching here—or bringing the lunch—something like that." She smiled brightly at Helen.

The shaft did not seem to penetrate. Helen said, "How lovely you look, Sonia. Blue is certainly your color, isn't it, Jake?"

He grunted something noncommittal and Sonia looked from Helen's worn jeans and sloppy shirt to the portrait of the smiling Spanish lady. "How lovely you were then. How can you bear to keep that around?"

"If you wear as well as Helen has," Jake began furiously, and his wife uttered an appalled "Jake!"

Sonia nodded to Janice. "If you are ready, darling, we might as well go."

How the creatures order one around here, Janice thought.

As they walked away, Sonia commented, "I hope you appreciate my rescuing you. Failures are such bores."

"Jake Peters isn't a failure."

Sonia disliked discussion or argument. As a woman she felt it wiser to be an appreciative audience; that was what men wanted. She dismissed Jake as of no interest. "I wanted to talk to you seriously about the cottage. Just as soon as Vladimir gets hold of you this afternoon, he is going to try to break down your resistance. He has ideas about changes he wants to make; extending the studio so there will be room enough to play quartets. He has a superstitious idea that the cottage works for him because what he has written here has been successful. And then," and she brooded, "he can keep an eye on me. That's half the charm of this place for him. I'm trapped in a cul-de-sac."

"I can't see you this afternoon, after all, so he won't have a chance to persuade me. I'm having dinner with Mrs. Nichols at six o'clock sharp. I couldn't refuse."

"If I know that woman, she never gave you a chance to refuse. And if you have any sense of self-preservation, darling, which I sometimes doubt, you'll watch your step. She gets worse all the time. She spends hours watching pictures of returning prisoners of war on television and about once a day she is sure she recognizes her son. It's downright eerie."

"Well, I've got to go tonight," Janice said in a tone of resignation, "but I'll try to make it clear that I never at any time intended to marry Lou. This thing has got to stop."

So it was in a mood of grim determination, in spite of her reluctance to meet either the mother or the son, that Janice was driven to the Nichols cottage that evening, taking with her a couple of bottles of wine from the Ransome supply.

"Pick me up at nine," she instructed Bertie. "Not a minute later."

There was a gleam of understanding in his face, but he said only, "Yes, Miss Edwards."

For once the cheese-paring Mrs. Nichols had the house lighted like a Christmas tree, both inside and out. The slam of the car door brought Thomas onto the porch but before he could reach Janice, his mother had brushed past him, crying in exultant tones, "Janice! Have you heard? Lou has been found! He'll be home next weekend. I told you so! I told you so."

II

Grace Nichols, usually slow-moving like her older son, grimly tenacious, single-minded, had flowered overnight. At first Janice suspected that, unlikely as it was, she was a trifle drunk, but she was merely in a state of overstimulation. Her usually flat voice was high and cracked with excitement; her eyes glittered; she waved her short arms to help her express her feelings.

"All this time! All this time! I knew he could not be dead. I always told you so."

The walls of the living room, like Mrs. Nichols's bedroom, in which Janice had left her coat, were covered with pictures of Lou—snapshots from the time he was a baby, through all the stages of growing up, to the young man whom Janice remembered. In all the pictures he was laughing. No one seeing the pictures would have guessed that Mrs. Nichols had two sons.

When she could make herself heard in a momentary lull in this unaccustomed torrent of speech, Janice asked, "But what happened? Why was he reported missing?"

"I don't know exactly. As soon as we got the news late last night, Thomas tried to find out. He's been on the telephone practically all night and all day. The important thing is that Lou will be back next weekend. In the morning I'll start turning out his room, the one Thomas has been using. You'll have to move into your father's old studio, Thomas. We can shift his desk and put in an army cot for you. I think I'll order one of those water beds for Lou. People seem to like them. Of course it would be only temporary, as he'll be marrying so soon. Maybe it would be a useless extravagance. What do you think, Janice?"

Janice turned to Thomas. "Please explain just what happened."

He revealed none of the ecstatic happiness shown by his mother. In fact, his expression was grim. "So far as I could make out," he said in a deliberate way, "Lou escaped from prison camp. He was apparently picked up by some friendly Vietnamese who sheltered him, God knows at what risk to themselves, until the fighting was over, when they got in touch with our forces."

"I'm going to order a big tenderloin steak for the night he comes home," his mother said happily, "with mushrooms and those roasted potatoes he likes and asparagus hollandaise and if there are any good strawberries in the market, I'll make a shortcake."

"Mother, I keep trying to tell you that Lou is in bad shape. After so many months of near starvation a heavy meal like that would probably make him sick, even if he could eat it at all."

"Well, but—we'll have something nice and with Janice here we'll celebrate with champagne. Or perhaps Janice will bring the champagne from the house. Mr. Ransome always had so much." She added thoughtfully, "And, of course, it's all Janice's now."

"You'd better wait until you see how Lou is. After that long trip and what he's been through, he may not feel like celebrating. He will want to be let alone. Wait awhile before you ask Janice to come to dinner."

"Janice's place is beside him if he should be ill. In sickness and in health. That's what it says."

"She isn't married to him yet." There was steel in Thomas's voice.

"Well, that could be arranged, of course. Thomas, you look into it and see what the formalities are for getting married in New York State."

"Mother!" For once his voice stopped her in midflight. "You've got to wait until Lou gets home. Let him decide what he wants."

"What he wants?" she repeated blankly.

"Hasn't it ever occurred to you that Lou might not want to marry Janice? Hasn't it ever occurred to you that he may have changed?"

FIVE

IT WAS, JANICE recognized later, the only thing that would have checked Mrs. Nichols in her single-minded determination to marry Janice to Lou. As it was, she agreed to wait until she ascertained Lou's wishes, and Janice decided to give Inspiration Lake a wide berth in the next few weeks. No doubt Lou would be able to convince his mother that he had no more desire to marry Janice than she to marry him.

Thomas, as she was well aware, was trying all evening to find a way to speak to her privately, but she did nothing to help him, joining his mother when she washed the dishes. The last thing she wanted at this point was to bring on a renewal of his proposal.

The early arrival of Bertie with the station wagon took him by surprise, but Mrs. Nichols was too happy to be as stubborn as usual and let her go without argument.

The news of the return of the missing POW had not only filtered through the little colony but it was known to everyone at the inn by the time the chartered plane took off for New York on Sunday evening. Before Thomas, who was hovering near the ramp, could reach her, Hal Streichen and his friend Bob Maxwell hailed her and again she found herself seated between them.

"I suppose," Hal said, "that Mrs. Nichols will kill the fatted calf for the returning hero."

"Apparently he is in bad health. She will probably have to postpone the celebration."

"I'm trying to persuade Bob to come up next weekend for some water-skiing, but he's backing out. And here I thought he was having himself a ball, dancing both Friday and Saturday nights with our Sonia." He gave Janice a malicious look. "It's a mistake to let this guy off the hook. Can't you persuade him, Janice?"

"I wish I could come back," Bob said regretfully. "There's nothing I would like better. But some people I work with can only be seen on weekends."

"Who are you kidding?" Hal scoffed.

"Whom." Janice corrected him.

"Listen to the bluestocking, will you? She et a book and it shows."

"It's true enough, unfortunately," Bob told him. "I can only see my people when it's convenient for them." He had a small importing firm, he explained to Janice. Then, with a disarming smile, he admitted, "Actually, I just have office space, a cubicle, one-fourth of a typist who also takes telephones calls for all us small-timers."

Getting started on a shoestring was always risky, so he had to see people when they were willing to see him and not at his own convenience.

"But I'll be thinking of you up there where it's cool."

"I'm not going up next weekend," Janice said.

He brightened. "Oh, in that case—"

Hal looked from one to the other and raised an eyebrow. From a seat across the aisle, Thomas too was watching them, his face set. As though it weren't bad enough to have his mother laying claim to me, Janice thought resentfully.

Next morning she was deep in a Gothic novel, in which a distraught heroine found herself imprisoned within decaying walls of the tower of an old chateau in France, held there by a sinister man of evil design to whom she was, nevertheless, irresistibly attracted, when she was aroused from this feverish dream by Fitz opening the door of his little office.

"It can't be all that good," he commented.

"Another Gothic," she said resentfully. "The only kind on which you trust my opinion."

He grinned at her. "Come in. I've got a problem here. A guy with a real talent but no cash to speak of to keep him going until he can write a book. I can give him a fifteen-hundred-dollar advance, but you know how it is: six months to write the book, another six months to publish, and still another six to find out whether it's even going to pay production costs. If I could only afford to up the ante, but the way costs are rising, I may have to sell out. I've had a fair offer from Universal."

"Oh, Fitz, you can't do that! You're building a good list, the kind you can be proud of. You've got one real prestige item for the spring list and a fair chance of a book club selection. Look, I hadn't meant to tell you, but I came into quite a packet of money unexpectedly and I put you down in my will for a hundred thousand to help keep the company going. You can just as well have it now if you want. The money's there."

"Well," he said slowly, "I'll be eternally damned! Come on in. I want you to meet Dave McClintock."

As the telephone on her desk jangled, Janice said, "Just a minute," and into the telephone, "Fitzgerald Publishing."

"Miss Edwards?" It was Bob's voice.

"Hello, Bob."

"How about dinner tonight?"

"I'd love to." Janice regretted the promptness of her answer. She might at least have pretended to consult her calendar.

"Where shall I pick you up?"

She gave him her address on East 54th Street.

"Apartment number?"

"It's the penthouse."

He whistled. "Hey, I hope you aren't too rich for my blood."

She laughed. "I'll see you at seven." She was still smiling when she went into the little office where Fitz, appearing longer than ever in contrast with a fair young man with sallow skin and hollow eyes, stood to greet her.

"Janice, this is Dave McClintock. Dave, Janice Edwards, my girl Friday. Sit down, Janice. We've got a problem. Dave is going to do a book for us about his experiences as a POW. Now here's where we have a problem. Dave is just out of prison camp and he needs someplace to stay away from the noise and the heat of the city until he can become a little more adjusted to civilian life. Can you dredge up any place in the country that is quiet and won't be too expensive?"

"Of course I can. Just the thing. Actually," Janice assured the bewildered young man. "I've been looking for someone like you." She turned to Fitz. "My stepfather bought a lake in the Adirondacks with a lot of land around it where he intended to establish an artist's colony, but he never carried out his plan. Anyhow, there are three unoccupied cottages right now and the lake is really lovely, cool and quiet, and there's complete privacy. Anyone interrupting any working artist is shot on sight. The cottages are rent-free, of course, for accredited workers in any of the arts. There's a woman, a Mrs. Peters, the wife of a painter, who would take you shopping once a week, if you will pay for the gas, or you could eat at the inn if you have a car or a bicycle to take you there."

Fitz shook his head in wonder. "You mean you've known about this place all the time and never breathed a word about it?"

"Well, it never happened to come up," she said apologetically.

"And you can get Dave into one of those cottages?"

"Of course. I own the place now. The inn, too; in fact, the whole lake."

"Of all the dark horses!" Still with that half-surprised, half-amused expression, Fitz turned to Dave. "How does it sound to you?"

"Unbelievable."

"Why," Janice suggested, "don't you go up to Inspiration Lake on Friday—there's always a chartered plane—spend the weekend at the inn as my guest and look at the vacant cottages? Mrs. Peters will show them to you and explain how the place is run, so you wouldn't feel that you were buying a pig in a poke."

"Having the pig given to me, roasted, served on a silver platter with an apple in its mouth," Dave corrected her. "I suppose things like this actually happen, but I've never encountered one before."

Over lunch at the Gotham, Fitz persuaded Dave to discuss his prison experiences. "It will loosen you up and get your thoughts oiled so you'll be all ready to start writing," he explained, but Janice saw that he was watching his young friend rather anxiously.

Even after having a cocktail and ordering a lavish meal—"For heaven's sake, eat up, man. You must be thirty pounds underweight"—Dave found it difficult to get started.

"What was the worst thing?" Fitz prompted him.

"Time. All those empty hours to get through. No news of the outside world, no idea how our side was doing, when or where this thing would ever end. Just time. I tried everything I could think of to fill it, but without books or paper and pencil it was a problem.

"Actually, except for rotten food and more rotten sanitary arrangements it wasn't too bad. I was beaten a couple of times but never tortured. On the whole we weren't treated much worse than the enemy's own men, the same lousy food, the same beatings. I never saw but one man tortured and that—"

Dave tackled his soup and buttered a roll lavishly. "That poor devil was one of those reckless guys who simply can't stand captivity or taking orders. He was always in trouble, even during the fighting. I know because we were in the same company. Anyhow, he got this idea that he could escape. None of us were willing to go along. There was nothing outside the camp but jungle. Jungle and snakes and the enemy. We were better off where we were. So when he asked us to go with him, he had no takers."

Dave relinquished his soup plate and started enthusiastically on prime ribs.

"Did he make it?" Fitz prodded him.

"No. He was caught at the wall as he was getting out." Dave's voice was deadly in its coldness. "One of us betrayed him."

"God! Why?"

"What did he get for it, you mean? I don't know."

"What happened to the guy who tried to escape?"

"He was tortured; the thing went on and on. I can still hear the poor devil screaming." Dave pushed his plate aside. "Even after the torture stopped—and I'm not going to describe that—he cried like a kid. He went on crying until we were all about crazy, and finally our captors pushed him out of the camp and that was the last I ever heard of him. Of course he died out there. Even if he had been in good condition there was practically no chance of survival alone in the jungle."

"And the other one? The Judas?"

"He got to be thick as thieves with the enemy. He was one of the first to be released and I'll bet," Dave snarled, "he got a hero's welcome on his return. If I ever lay hands on him, he's one man I intend to kill."

"Don't be a fool," Fitz warned him sharply. "Eat up, man." He pushed Dave's plate back.

"The damnable thing," Dave said, "was that the three of us had been drafted at the same time, got our basic training together, got shipped out together, got captured together. We had shared all that. So you can understand maybe why I said—"

"No," Fitz snapped. "No. Forget it, Dave. It's the past."

It was late in the afternoon when Janice brought the contract for Fitz's approval. He went through it quickly and said, "Good girl! And thank you for providing a place for Dave to work in."

"There's no need to thank me. This whole thing fell into my lap and I'm delighted to find someone to make use of one of the vacant cottages. I had meant to ask if you knew of anyone who rated or needed such a place."

"How come, with all those shekels, you are willing to work for peanuts?"

"I like the job and I like having something interesting to do. Anyhow," Janice smiled, "I get so many lovely Gothics to read."

"Go on improving," he told her gravely, "and you'll graduate to mysteries. After that the sky's the limit. At least, when you learn how to spell."

"I used to think life could hold no more than the leisure to read romantic novels all day long."

"But the charm didn't last?"

"I'm like the Lady of Shalott, 'half-sick of shadows,'" and then Janice laughed at herself.

"As I recall my Tennyson, that was when the young lovers came into her ken, wasn't it?" Before Janice could reply, Fitz said, "I'm glad you'll have a chance to show Dave the ropes up at this lake of yours."

"I'm not going up next weekend or, probably, for some time, not until a rather disturbing situation can be straightened out." She looked at her watch and covered her typewriter.

"Why don't you have a drink with me this afternoon?"

It was the first invitation she had received from him, except for the daily lunches at the Gotham during which they either discussed authors or entertained authors and agents. She wondered why he was bothering now but assumed it was gratitude for finding a solution for his friend.

"Thank you but I have a date and I'll have to rush. I want to change."

"A heavy date?"

"Well, middleweight." She laughed, picked up her handbag and went out, walking with the new confidence she had acquired. Fitz looked after her, frowning. Then he pulled a script toward him and made a marginal note.

II

Bob's eyes lighted up when he saw Janice standing in the doorway of the penthouse, wearing a long dress of soft gray. She stood aside to let him go through the entrance and into the big living room, one wall of which was made up of windows.

He whistled. "This is terrific."

"Come see." She led the way out on the terrace. There were tables, chairs, beach umbrellas, trees in tubs, several rosebushes whose blossoms scented the air, and even a strip of grass. The view, from fifteen floors above the ground, was breathtaking. In the background soared the towers of lower Manhattan, in the middle distance rose the Empire State Building, and to the west the Rockefeller Center complex. Below tugboats moved sluggishly up and down the East River, the hoarse blast of their whistles muted at this height.

"How did you ever manage to get this?" Bob demanded when they were seated on long chairs on the terrace.

"Theda Ferrell bought the penthouse while she was playing *Forever Mary*, which had such a long run in New York. Then she offered it to me when she went to Rome to make a picture. I'd closed up my stepfather's town house and it seemed ideal, especially as I didn't know how much I'd have to live on and she was letting me have this rent-free. Then she married a man with a monstrous fortune and they're going to live permanently in Switzerland to avoid taxes, so I've decided to buy the penthouse. It's silly, of course, all this room for one person, but I think it's fun. And you should see it after dark. Artificial moonlight. Honestly!"

"I hope to see it after dark. Lots and lots of times." Then Bob added in chagrin, "But I didn't know you had all this. I'm just beginning to get on my feet."

"Does that matter?"

His face lighted. "I hope not."

That was an evening to remember, not that anything

special happened. They had dinner at a moderately priced restaurant, where Bob refused to discuss his war experiences—all that, he said firmly, was behind him—but talked instead of his boyhood on a farm in a singularly united and happy family. She expressed her envy and described her disinherited girlhood, not with self-pity but with an ironic detachment. It had just been one of those things.

Later, after an enjoyable movie, Janice asked him to come up for a nightcap and see the moonlight. The magical effect was all that she claimed for it.

"Phony, of course," he agreed, "but nice phony. I like it." And, whether it was the moonlight or not, he kissed her, lightly, gently, and asked, "How soon can I see you again?"

He came Tuesday, Wednesday, and Thursday. Each evening they talked more about themselves. Bob told her how the farm had burned down, both his father and mother being overcome by smoke and dying in the farmhouse before they could be reached. He and his brother Bruce had escaped. Today his brother had a good job in Brazil, but it was a long way off, of course, and he couldn't afford to make the trip.

"Actually," he explained, anxious to make his situation clear to her. "I can't afford the prices at the inn up at your lake. Hal Streichen took me along as his guest, and thank heaven for that. Otherwise I'd never have met you. Do you go up every weekend?"

"I'm not going tomorrow," Janice was embarrassed. She sounded as though she expected him to see her every night.

He brightened. "Oh, good."

"I thought you had to see some men on business this weekend."

"That was just for Hal's consumption. Nice guy and all that but a little of him goes a long way. You'll be spending a lot of time at the lake this summer, I suppose." The prospect seemed to give him no pleasure.

"I certainly won't go more often than I have to, though

there are a lot of details to be decided on. A woman up there has a fixed idea that I am going to marry her son."

After a pause he said blankly, "I didn't know."

"He is the man from Vietnam who was reported missing."

"Oh, that one."

"Yes, that one. He's to be home this weekend, so I thought I'd give the place a wide berth for a while, at least until Lou can convince his mother that he's no more interested in me than I am in him."

"And he isn't?"

"Of course not."

He smiled down at her. He was one of the few men she knew tall enough to do that, except lanky Fitz. "There's no 'of course' about it. You aren't a girl a man would easily forget, if that's what you are counting on, Janice. You wouldn't let yourself be pressured out of pity or anything like that?"

The telephone was ringing as she emptied a tray of ice. "Answer it, Bob, will you? I'll be there in just a minute."

She emptied the tray into an ice bucket and went to the telephone to find Bob setting it down, a look of bewilderment on his face.

"What goes on here?" he demanded.

"Who was it?"

"The damnedest thing! A woman said, 'Who are you?' And when I told her I was Robert Maxwell, she asked what I was doing here and then she said, 'Well, you have no business being there, whoever you are. Janice is going to marry my son. I want her to come up this weekend. You tell her so.' And she hung up."

"Oh, dear," Janice exclaimed in dismay. "Oh, dear."

"But you aren't going?"

"No, I am certainly not going."

"Thank God for that." Bob strolled back to the terrace with her and mixed the cocktails. He handed her a frosty glass and lifted his own. "To us," he said.

And Janice, smiling, echoed, "To us."

SIX

"IT WOULD BE nice," Fitz remarked mildly, as he laid a manuscript on Janice's desk, "if you could come down to earth for a few minutes."

Janice, who had been lost in thought, looked up at him with a start.

"May I know how long this state of euphoria is going to last?"

"All my life, I hope."

He was startled. "You aren't serious!"

"I couldn't be more serious."

"My God, you aren't going to leave me now I've got you nicely broken in?"

She laughed and shook her head. "No, I'd like to go on working. I enjoy the job and, anyhow, with Bob busy all day long I'll need something to occupy me, and I can't help him because I don't know anything about the importing business."

There was naked shock in Fitz's face. "You mean this has reached the stage where you are talking marriage?"

Janice gave him a mischievous smile and extended her left hand on which there was a wedding ring. "I was married day before yesterday." As Fitz was speechless, she said, "It was all in a rush. A lot of factors entered into it. We were sure in our own minds about ourselves and each other, we neither of us wanted an elaborate wedding. I have no family and he has only one brother, who lives in Brazil, and then there were other things—"

"Go on." Fitz settled himself on the edge of her desk, watching her expression intently.

"There's a woman up at the lake who has an obsession about my marrying her son. I hoped when Lou came back from the service he would tell her that he wasn't interested in me, but it seems that he's not well and now she expects me to marry him and take care of him. Of course, sooner or later, I'll have to go back to the lake, but I'll postpone it as long as possible."

"Speaking of the lake, Dave telephoned. He is coming down on the morning plane to talk about the book. He is crazy about the cottage; he thinks it is a perfect setup."

"Well, it could be if it weren't for Mrs. Nichols spoiling everything. So when Bob and I talked it over, we decided that it would be better to marry quietly and without fuss, and then, if we have to see her at all, it will be with a *fait accompli.* So we got married on Wednesday, which is why I couldn't join you for lunch and meet the Fredericks woman. Well, we'd made our plans and then, as luck would have it, Bob got an urgent call to attend a meeting of some kind in Atlantic City. He was terribly upset, but it may mean something really important for him so, of course, I told him he ought to go. He left right after the wedding."

As the door opened, she turned inquiringly and then turned back to silence the telephone. "Fitzgerald Publishing." Her face lighted up, her voice warmed. "Bob! . . . You are leaving now? O frabjous day! . . . Yes, lunch at the Gotham at one." As Fitz slid off her desk, she shook her head, spoke a few more words, and then turned to smile at him. "Bob made some wonderful contacts. . . . Oh don't wince. Lots of people say it. And he's getting on a bus in Atlantic City this very minute. I want you to meet him."

She was too engrossed in her thoughts to observe that Fitz showed no overwhelming desire to meet Bob Maxwell. She forgot about the opening of the door. No one had come in and the door had been quietly closed again.

By half-past twelve she found herself unable to concentrate on anything. Her eyes kept going back to her watch hands that seemed to stand still.

Dave McClintock arrived and shook hands with her warmly. "You've given me the biggest break I ever had. The cottage is ideal and the lake is lovely. I've already settled down to a writing schedule, but I want to check with Fitz before I get too far into the book and make sure I'm on the right track. If I can ever find a way of paying back—"

"You don't owe me a thing. The place was designed for people like you."

Hearing their voices, Fitz came out to greet Dave. "I thought I recognized those dulcet tones. Ready for lunch? How about you, Janice?"

"I'll wait for Bob."

And at last the door opened and Bob stood there, big and broad-shouldered and smiling. He came to take her in his arms, and when he finally released her, flushed and smiling and breathless, he said, "At last, Mrs. Maxwell."

"How was the convention? But I don't need to ask. I've never seen you look so—so relaxed. So triumphant."

"The convention was fabulous, but the triumph has a different reason. Can't you guess?"

She laughed. "Tell me about the convention."

"Later. We've got all the time in the world from now on. Think of that! Let's go out to lunch. I'm starving."

As the headwaiter at the Gotham started toward Fitz's regular table, Janice stopped him. "We're lunching alone today." She saw Fitz look up from the big menu and waved at him. He nodded and looked searchingly at Bob, trying to appraise the man who had swept her off her feet. He would find nothing to criticize in Bob, she thought proudly.

"Champagne cocktails?" Bob suggested. "We never have had a proper wedding celebration."

"Fine! Bob, the tall thin man sitting with the smaller

one over there is Fitz, my boss. Oh, you can't see him without turning around. Never mind, you'll be meeting him."

When the champagne cocktails came, they toasted each other, smiling, gay and confident. They were dawdling over coffee when Fitz and Dave went past. After looking from one to the other, Dave put out a hand to check Fitz, who was about to stop, and led him out. How considerate he was, Janice thought, and promptly forgot him.

In a few minutes a page came into the room intoning, "Mr. Maxwell. Mr. Robert Maxwell."

Bob raised his head alertly, a frown of surprise drawing his brows together. "No one knows I am here."

"Mr. Maxwell. Mr. Robert Maxwell."

"I am Robert Maxwell."

"Telephone call. You can take it at the desk in the lobby."

Bob fumbled for a coin, said, "Be right back," and left Janice alone. He was back in a few minutes, with the laughter and the triumph wiped from his face. "Darling, it's the damnedest thing. First I leave you on our wedding day; now I've got to leave you in the midst of our wedding luncheon."

"Oh, no! What's wrong?"

"It's my brother Bruce. At least, it must be Bruce. A long-distance call from Brazil, but I could hardly make out a word, what with a lot of the talk being in Portuguese and a bad connection. So far as I could gather, something has happened to my brother."

"I'm so sorry. What are you going to do?"

"Go to the Brazilian consulate and see what the quickest procedure would be to get some reliable information. I'll see you at the penthouse. Okay?"

He had been moving his things there, bit by bit, since Monday, and had completed moving on Wednesday, the morning they were married.

"Do you have your key?"

He tapped his pocket. "Key to paradise," he said unexpectedly, touched her hand, and then he was gone.

Janice swallowed her disappointment. So far her marriage had been a series of disappointments. Not that Bob wanted to be unreasonable. The convention had been vital to his interests and, of course, he would be worried about his brother.

So she drifted back to the office, feeling disconsolate. Fitz and Dave were talking at her desk and broke off when she came in. With a nod to Fitz, Dave went out.

Fitz raised his brows. "Where is Benedick the married man?"

"He was paged at the Gotham, a mixed-up telephone call from Brazil, where his brother lives. Apparently something has happened and Bob went to the consulate to see how to get some news."

Fitz propped a bony shoulder against the wall. In profile the big nose dominated his face, but in full face his smile was engaging. He was not smiling now. He looked down at the scuffed linoleum on the floor. "So that's your husband."

Janice nodded happily. "I was sorry you didn't stop to meet him. You'll like him. But Mr. McClintock is so considerate. I know he didn't want to interrupt us."

Fitz started to speak, changed his mind, and went back to his office. In a moment Janice heard a drawer crash shut. It was unlike Fitz to lose his temper. A short time later he came out saying curtly, "I won't be back this afternoon. Call it a day if you like. Mustn't keep the bridegroom waiting."

II

The apartment building in which Janice lived had an impressive lobby but a self-service elevator, with the desk and switchboard around the corner. Surely Bob would be home by now.

"Bob?" she called, when she had unlocked the door. "Bob?"

But there was no answer. There was no one in the

apartment. The towels in the bathroom were unused, though the room was not as neat as usual. The maid supplied by the management of the building was not as efficient as the one Janice had employed. But when, on Tuesday, she had found bronze hairpins on her dressing table and on a pillow slip, and discovered that some of the exquisite embroidered linen handkerchiefs her mother had given her were missing, she had dismissed the girl. The maid, first tearful and then angry, denied having taken the handkerchiefs, denied that she had made use of Janice's dressing table and Janice's bed.

"You'll find it was someone else," she had said before slamming out of the apartment, but, of course, there could have been no one else. No one could get into the apartment. True, Janice had lost her key some time before and had to have it replaced, but no stranger picking it up would know to whom it belonged or what door it fitted.

When she had switched on the air conditioning and had changed to a new and becoming housecoat, she set the table on the terrace with a lace tablecloth, got out cocktail things and fixed a tray, filled the bucket with ice and plunged a stately bottle of champagne into it.

She opened a package of frozen lobster and left it to defrost, and prepared a Newburg sauce, measured out coffee, and put rolls in a pan ready to heat. Then she sat down to wait.

She waited a long time, waited until the sun set and the lights of the city performed their nightly magic. Waited until she was chilly and went inside for a wrap, switching on the artificial moonlight when she returned. As she passed the cocktail tray, she mixed herself a martini and sipped it slowly, wondering what could possibly have happened to Bob. Twice the telephone rang, but once it was a wrong number and once a handicapped woman who asked her to buy hosiery.

She mixed a second drink. By now she was shivering. Something had happened to Bob. He would never have let her wait like this without getting a message to her somehow, unless he was hurt, so badly hurt he couldn't talk.

At length she looked up the number of the Brazilian consulate, but an answering service informed her that the office had closed for the night.

When she had exhausted herself pacing the floor, she looked up the number of Bob's office. She glanced at her watch. For the hundredth time? The thousandth time? It was nine-thirty. Probably no one would be there. Certainly no one would be there. Nonetheless she dialed the number.

"Far East Imports," a voice said.

"Is Mr. Maxwell there?"

"Mr. Maxwell is attending a convention in Atlantic City. May I know who is calling?"

"No, he returned to New York at noon. This is his wife speaking."

"Who?"

"Mrs. Maxwell. He expected to be home before dinner and I haven't heard from him. I'm terribly anxious."

"Home," the girl said. "This is news to me. He never breathed a word about getting married. Where is home, if you don't mind my asking?"

Janice gave her the address and telephone number. "We were married the morning he had to leave for Atlantic City. If you should hear from him, please tell him—oh never mind." She put down the telephone.

At ten o'clock she got up stiffly and cleared away the supper she had prepared, picked up the ice bucket and then, with a wry smile, opened the bottle, hearing a fine satisfactory pop, and poured herself a bubbling glass. She raised it. "To the married happiness of Mr. and Mrs. Robert Maxwell." She drained the glass and then deliberately smashed it against the waist-high wall that fenced in the terrace.

When the ring came at the door at half-past ten, the combination of two martinis, one glass of champagne, and practically no food since breakfast, as she had been too excited to eat her lunch, made her stagger slightly as she went to the door.

There were two big men, middle-aged, with hard, weather-beaten faces and sober expressions, waiting.

"Mrs. Maxwell?"

It was the first time anyone had called her that except for Bob. She nodded mutely. Her throat closed when she saw their expressions. As she stepped back, they moved forward until they were inside and one of them closed the door.

"Mrs. Maxwell, we are sorry to inform you—"

One of them eased her into a chair. Even in her dazed condition she was aware that they must know she had been drinking, but it seemed to be more trouble than it was worth to explain. Anyhow, it didn't matter. Nothing mattered. Because Bob was dead. That was what they had come to tell her. Bob had jumped or fallen or been pushed from a window in the midtown Grand Hotel on Seventh Avenue, a most unlikely place for him to have been. He had been found shortly after two-thirty in the afternoon.

"Then it must have happened just after he left me! I don't understand. He was going to the Brazilian consulate."

The delay in making the identification was due to the fact that there was nothing on him: no billfold, no papers of any kind. His fingerprints had been identified by the FBI because of his army service, and they had found his business address in the telephone book and talked to the woman who ran a kind of community answering and typing service for four men, each of whom rented desk space. Fortunately she had been working late, typing a long price estimate for one of her clients, and she had told them that a Mrs. Maxwell had just called to find out where her husband was. The girl seemed to be greatly surprised to know that Mr. Maxwell was married.

"Are you all right?" one of the detectives asked, bending over and speaking loudly and distinctly as though she were deaf or mentally deficient.

"I'm all right," she said slowly, "or perhaps I'm a little drunk. I don't know. Bob didn't come and I haven't eaten and I had a cocktail. Two cocktails."

"Suppose," one of the detectives said, "you have some coffee," and the men accompanied her to the kitchen, where she plugged in the coffeepot she had filled so many hours ago for Bob, who would never be coming home.

When she had drunk some coffee and eaten a buttered roll at the urging of one of the men, she was able to look at them more clearly, to think more clearly. She explained the hasty marriage and said that Bob had been called to a convention in Atlantic City; he had taken a bus back to New York that morning and they planned to have lunch at the Gotham at one o'clock.

"And he came, and we had lunch, and then someone paged him. A telephone call that upset him horribly. He'd got a mixed-up message from Brazil, where his only brother Bruce lives. He couldn't make head or tail of it. He was going to the Brazilian consulate and he'd meet me here. But he never came. He said there was no hurry. He said we had all the rest of our lives." Her voice cracked.

Over her head the two men exchanged glances. Better get it over before she broke down. "We hate to ask you this, but, as a formality, will you come to the morgue and identify the body? Of course, we have checked the fingerprints but—still—there are some odd features."

So Janice went on wooden legs to change to a dark dress and pick up her handbag. When she returned, the two men broke off a low-toned conversation and stood up politely.

"But what," she asked, when she was seated in the police car, "was Bob doing in that hotel? I can't understand it at all."

"We don't know yet, but we'll find out. Mrs. Maxwell, did your husband have any enemies?"

"I don't see how he could have," she said naïvely; "he was such a—well, at least I don't know of any enemy, and he never spoke of one."

"What about his friends?"

"The only one I know is Hal Streichen. I met Bob when Hal took him up to the inn at Inspiration Lake for a weekend." She gave them Hal's address. "But I don't think he could help you. He never really takes enough interest in anyone, except in the way of gossip, to be useful."

She got out of the car without assistance and walked into the room where the body lay on a table, covered by a sheet. The detectives ranged themselves on either side of her, waiting for the inevitable collapse.

Then the attendant drew back the sheet and Janice stood looking down. Just as one of the detectives reached out to grasp her arm, she stepped back.

"That isn't Bob," she said. "That isn't my husband. I never saw him before."

SEVEN

THERE WAS A moment's silence in the cold room and then one of the detectives spoke to the attendant in a low voice. The latter gave the girl a quick, appraising look and then, leaning over, pulled off the toupé that made the man appear bald, detached the goatee, and, thrusting a finger inside the cheeks, removed some lumps of cotton.

Janice stared at the quiet face, so astonished that she was not even aware of shock. Yes, that was her husband. But why? Shortly before two o'clock he had left her at the Gotham to go to the Brazilian consulate. Half an hour later, wearing a disguise, he had fallen to his death from a room in a commercial hotel. Why?

"That," one of the detectives said, "is what we want to know. You positively identify this man as your husband, Robert Maxwell?"

"Yes. Oh, yes." She braced herself against the metal edge of the table, looking at the queerly twisted neck, at the face empty of expression, empty of color, empty of life.

And at last they took her home. "We'll want to see you later, of course, Mrs. Maxwell. There are bound to be a number of questions."

"I know. The thing is that I don't seem to have any answers."

"Don't think about it now," one of the men said fatuously as they left her at the door of the penthouse.

Don't think about it. At five in the morning she was still staring at the ceiling, lying rigid in bed, wondering why? Why? Why? What had happened in that half hour when Bob had plunged to his death from a room in a midtown hotel? Bob in disguise. Bob murdered. It had been a kind of freak accident, one of the men had told her. The body had been crushed and the skull cracked, but the face had been unharmed and undisfigured.

It was the telephone call, of course, that had lured him to his death, and he must have known that he was in danger. Otherwise the disguise was meaningless. Who had hated him enough to push him out of a window and how had anyone managed to do it? Hardly one man alone. Bob was big and strong and tough. He would have put up a terrific fight. Somehow she was sure of that.

"We have all the time in the world," he had assured her.

And at last she found relief in tears.

II

The story had broken too late for the early editions of the morning papers, but it was on radio and television. There wasn't much in the first accounts. Robert Maxwell, importer, aged thirty, had jumped or fallen to his death from a room in the Grand Hotel at half-past two on Friday afternoon. Apparently he had been robbed, as there were no papers on the body, which had been identified by his fingerprints. He was survived by his wife. The strangest element in the case was the fact that the victim was wearing a disguise.

It was not until afternoon, when enterprising reporters had done their homework, that the story became more important. Mrs. Robert Maxwell, widow of the man who had plunged to his death from a window in the Grand Hotel, was a bride of less than a week and the former Janice Edwards, sole heiress of the estate of her stepfather, the late Carl Ransome, financier and art patron.

By that time the telephone was ringing steadily. There were reporters, acquaintances, and the cranks who had had a mystic vision to explain the whole tragedy. After a time Janice shut off the telephone, grateful for the gadget her predecessor had installed to mute the bell. She called the desk and left word that she would accept only official calls.

"Yes, Miss Edwards. I mean Mrs. Maxwell," a flustered voice said.

It was midafternoon before she was able to eat a slice of toast and drink a couple of cups of coffee, but that light meal made her feel a bit more competent when the house phone rang.

"It's some men from the police."

The two men whom she admitted were unknown to her. They looked her over carefully and looked at the great living room, which air conditioning made comfortable in spite of the sweltering heat of the city. A lot of money somewhere. Money had a way of showing up in these cases.

"I wish we didn't have to disturb you, Mrs. Maxwell," the older man said, after looking at the tall girl in the dark dress, whose eyes looked enormous in a face that was somehow shrunken, whose white lips twitched.

"Of course, it's all right. Any way I can help you. Only," she made an empty gesture, "I don't know anything. I'm completely bewildered."

"Well," he said in an easy, relaxed tone that made her aware her voice was too shrill, "there are a lot of things we'd like to know, of course. To begin with, what can you tell me about your husband's family?"

"There is no one but a brother Bruce who lives in Brazil, and that is all I know about him. They have always been devoted, though they haven't met in some time."

"You don't know where he lives? In what city?"

She shook her head.

The lieutenant, whose name was Carrigan and who seemed to have too many teeth in his mouth, thought: She marries a guy without knowing anything about his family or his background. And all that money just waiting to be picked up by the first smooth operator who comes along. That girl shouldn't have been allowed out alone. Aloud he said, "Trying to find a Bruce Maxwell in a country as big as Brazil is like looking for the proverbial needle. But we'll do our best, of course."

The younger man, Tim Jackson, with a sharp nose and eyes too close together but with an unexpected and disarming dimple in his cheek, took notes.

"What about your husband's business?"

"He was just starting out. He had invested in a small importing company called Far East Imports. That's why he had to go away just after we were married to attend a convention in Atlantic City. When he got back, he told me it had been fabulous and he looked that way. Jubilant." She managed to steady her voice.

"We'll be talking to Mr. Maxwell's typist later on."

"I'd like to see her, too. There's so little I know, so much I want to know." Janice got up to answer the house phone, a call for Lieutenant Carrigan.

After listening a few minutes, he said, "That's an odd one. What do you think?" Listened again, said, "Hold on."

He came back into the room. "That was the precinct, Mrs. Maxwell. A Mrs. Bruce Maxwell is there. She has something to say and she would like to meet you, too."

"You mean she's Bob's sister-in-law? Then I'd like very much to see her. Perhaps she would care to come here."

"If you say so." With a measuring look he went back to the telephone, suggested that Mrs. Bruce Maxwell come to the penthouse, and called the desk to leave instructions that she was to be sent up on her arrival.

"Then she must be the one who called Bob yesterday," Janice said. "I didn't even know Bruce was married. Bob couldn't have known she was in town or she'd have been invited to the wedding. Or perhaps she has just arrived."

"Or perhaps," interjected the younger man, "she checked in at room twelve-seventeen at the Grand Hotel." As Janice looked a question, he explained, "That's the room from which your husband fell to his death. We've learned that much. Whoever took the room registered in the name of M. Canning. No one remembers—but who could in a place like that with people coming and going all the time—whether it was a man or a woman. Does the name mean anything to you?"

"Canning?" Janice repeated the name as though savoring it on her tongue. She shook her head. "Not a thing. How did you discover which room it was?"

"A window wide open. A hammer on the floor which was the murder weapon, plenty of evidence of that, but no fingerprints. His skull was cracked, you know. If it's any comfort to you, he was dead before he went out of the window." The younger detective wondered whether she was listening. There was a curiously blank look as though she was still in shock.

When it became apparent to the lieutenant that the widow had no information to give him about her husband—I wouldn't buy a dog I knew that little about, he thought—he suggested that while they awaited Mrs. Bruce Maxwell, they examine Mr. Maxwell's effects. Janice led the way to the spare bedroom which had been turned over to Bob. There were clothes stacked on the bed, shoes in a pile on the floor, and a jumble of miscellaneous items, including shaving gear, on the dresser.

She returned to the living room and stood staring sightlessly out of the window until the sergeant came back.

"Have you gone through your husband's things?"

She turned in surprise. "No, of course not."

"Well, someone has," he told her, and went back to resume his examination.

Janice looked after him, a faint frown on her face. Then she dismissed the idea as unlikely. There was no one who even knew that Bob's clothes and personal effects were in the apartment, and anyhow, no one could have gotten in.

When the two-toned bell rang, the policemen returned and Janice went to admit a young woman who gave her a quick look and then walked into the room. She was older than Janice, perhaps twenty-eight, with brassy blond hair that was dark at the roots. She was too thin and her skin was a bad color. She wore a white trouser suit with a red blouse, high-heeled red shoes, and she carried an outsize red plastic handbag.

Janice held out her hand. "Bruce's wife? I'm so glad to know you."

The girl took her hand, looking faintly surprised, and then she caught her breath as she looked around her. "Jeez! It's just like the movies."

"Mrs. Maxwell, this is Lieutenant Carrigan. Sergeant Jackson. Please sit down."

The girl dropped onto a tapestried chair, still looking around her. "Well, this is something! Bob really fell into a good thing. But he didn't get to enjoy it long, did he?" She laughed harshly.

"Mrs. Maxwell!" the lieutenant protested, shocked while Janice gaped at her, too astonished to comment.

"Look, Fuzz," Mrs. Bruce Maxwell said, "let's don't weep any crocodile tears about my brother-in-law. I hated his guts." She whirled on Janice. "And you may not know it yet, but you are lucky. If he'd had the chance, he'd have smashed things up for you the way he did for me."

Before Janice could reply, she rushed on. "He set up a phony adultery scene for me, pictures and everything, so Bruce could get a divorce and marry this middle-aged widow from Brazil. Loaded, she was. Emeralds. Coffee. I don't know what all. But he wouldn't have done anything if Bob hadn't interfered. And what happens to me?" Her voice had risen to a thin scream. "I'll tell you. No training. No education to speak of. So what am I doing? I work in the cleaning end of a laundromat. Steaming hot all day long and in this weather. That's what I'm doing. So if someone threw Bob out of a window, I say more power to whoever did it."

She was shaking with anger. "Bruce always did what Big Brother told him. But I guess they were the same breed at that. Gutter rats from Mott Street, who clawed their way up in the world out of a lousy slum. But they were smart, you have to give them that. To hear them talk, you wouldn't guess about their background unless they got mad. Then it showed. But they could talk real nice when they put their minds to it."

Janice swallowed. "Mrs. Maxwell—"

"Look, dearie, we're sisters under the skin, like the man says, so call me Bessie. It's all in the family, you know."

Lieutenant Carrigan intervened. "Mrs. Maxwell, where were you yesterday afternoon? Say from one to four?"

Bessie Maxwell blinked at him and then she clutched at the arms of her chair, her color mottled. "Look, just what are you trying to put over on me, you dirty pig? I haven't laid eyes on Bob in a long time, not since he went into the army."

"Where were you?" he repeated.

She clenched her hands. "Of all the lousy breaks. Friday is my day off because we work long hours on Saturday—and it's costing me plenty to take this time off, I can tell you. I went to the movies because it was cool there and my room is like an oven, nearly a hundred in the middle of the afternoon."

"I see. Where did you go?"

"Trans-Lux on Forty-eighth Street."

"What did you see?"

She moistened her lips. At last she said in an exhausted voice, "It was cool like I said. You know? And I was bushed. I fell asleep."

When she left, after having written down her address and the name of her employer, all her bravado gone, Carrigan said, "What a fool that woman is! Get on it, Sergeant. Check that sample of her handwriting with the registration at the Grand Hotel. Find out what you can about her background."

"You know," Janice intervened, "I believed her. If she had—killed Bob, she would have been prepared for your questions. She would have had a better alibi than that."

"She hated your husband, ma'am."

"Yes, I can see that she did. I suppose it is easier to blame someone else than yourself for your misfortunes."

"It won't be hard to check on the divorce," Carrigan said.

"But you can't be sure of what the real circumstances were. I wish—the poor thing has to go back to that hot room and the laundromat—I wish I had thought to ask her to stay here."

"Good God!" Carrigan exclaimed. "You can't do that, ma'am. We don't know yet whether she had any part in your husband's death, and she's not a good person to have here. We don't want you going over that wall," and he nodded toward the terrace, with a sheer drop of fifteen floors to the ground. "For your husband's killer that would be a natural, ma'am."

"Don't." Janice choked as she pictured Bob, falling, falling, his helpless body twisting and turning in the air, striking the sidewalk.

"You all right?" the sergeant asked.

She nodded. "I was just imagining—" Her voice trailed off. Then she took a deep breath. "But that girl couldn't possibly have pushed Bob out of a window! Not possibly. He was big and strong and in fine condition and she's just a little thing and underweight."

"A little girl with a big hammer. Well, maybe she's in the clear. We aren't jumping at anything. On the other hand we've got a woman who hated your husband's guts and is glad he is dead—a woman who had a powerful motive if she was telling the truth."

"But killing Bob wouldn't have brought Bruce back to her. Not if he has remarried."

"It's early days yet. We'll let you rest now, ma'am."

When Janice opened the door for them, a messenger who had been about to ring the bell thrust a long box of roses into her hands, saying, "Mrs. Maxwell?" A card fell off and the lieutenant picked it up, read it, his brows arching, and handed it to Janice without comment.

It read: "All my sympathy. Please make use of me in any way at any time for any purpose. Fitz."

EIGHT

WHILE SHE arranged the long-stemmed roses, Janice had no thoughts to spare for their donor. She was trying to come to terms with the accusations made by Bob's unlikely sister-in-law. Even discrediting the account of her divorce, and the chances were that she was eager to clear herself and cast the blame on someone else, her spontaneous reaction to the penthouse and Bob's good luck in acquiring it through marriage had sounded genuine. And the contrast between her picture of Bob's background and his own, between the happy family on the farm and the rat-infested Mott Street slum out of which he had clawed his way could not have been greater.

When the telephone rang, she went eagerly to answer it. Lieutenant Carrigan had promised to let her be present when he interviewed the woman who typed and took telephone calls for Bob.

"You understand," the lieutenant said over the phone, "that it is unlikely she'll have much to tell us because she worked for him only a few months. But if you would like to question her yourself, you'd better come now, as she has already put in a lot of overtime and she is extremely anxious to get home."

"There may be something to learn. I'll get there as quickly as possible."

"Remember there are newsmen waiting outside your building. You needn't answer any questions. Just say 'No comment' and walk on."

Janice put on dark glasses, tied a scarf around her head, and picked up two of her most brightly colored dresses, which she hung over her arm as though taking them to a cleaner. She took the service elevator and went out through the areaway. A group of men and women turned sharply as she came out of the service entrance, glanced at them indifferently, and strolled past. At a delicatessen around the corner, which she occasionally patronized, she explained her predicament and asked if she might leave the dresses for an hour or so. The owner, pleased to have even a minor role in the drama, agreed with alacrity and Janice, removing scarf and dark glasses, went out to hail a cab.

The office building was a run-down affair with an ancient creaking elevator. The operator was dozing on a bench against the wall, a racing form at his feet. He blinked sleepily at her.

"Who you want to see? Most of the offices are closed for the weekend."

"Far East Imports."

That awakened him. "Nice goings-on," he said in disapproval. "A tenant got himself killed and the police are there now. Sure you want to go up?" When Janice nodded, he had her sign the book and took her to the fifth floor.

There were some small cubicles, each equipped with a desk, telephone, and a couple of chairs. Near the door there was a switchboard and a desk with a typewriter. A group of men hovered outside one of the cubicles which someone was dusting for fingerprints, while another man was going through the desk drawers. The latter, Lieutenant Carrigan, looked up as he heard the elevator door slam.

"Mrs. Maxwell, this is Mrs. Pia Jensen, a typist who also takes telephone calls for the men who rent desk space here. We have gone ahead, checking Mr. Maxwell's desk and the list of telephone calls he made and received, but we waited to question Mrs. Jensen until you came, as I know you are anxious to learn all you can. Suppose we sit over here," and he indicated an unoccupied cubicle to which a sergeant pulled up chairs and then settled himself with an open notebook before him.

Mrs. Jensen was a blonde, not synthetic like Bessie Maxwell, but the genuine article, with heavy straight hair the color of honey in a thick braid worn like a crown, and handsome Scandinavian features. She was in her late twenties and wore tight slacks and a pale green blouse that outlined her heavy breasts.

"Mrs. Jensen," Lieutenant Carrigan began, and she looked away from Janice, whom she had been studying curiously, and answered his questions clearly and without hesitation. Her address was in the Bronx. She was divorced.

"When my husband learned that our little girl had polio and that she would be a big expense from now on, he walked out on us." She shrugged. "He was still just a kid, so I guess you can't blame him."

"But what about you?" Janice demanded in some indignation.

"A mother is different. Mothers don't walk out. Well, I guess they do at that, but little Karen is real sweet and she's too young yet to know how bad it is going to be for her later on. She has a break coming. I've got a real nice woman to look after her during the day, a retired schoolteacher who is giving her a real good start before she goes to school."

She pulled out a cigarette and a strip of matches. "You didn't ask me to wait here all Saturday afternoon just to talk about my little girl."

"You know, of course, what happened to Mr. Maxwell."

She nodded, and again she flicked a look at Janice, a measuring look in which there was also a tinge of amusement. "Oh, sure. The police called me here last night just after Mrs. Maxwell had called. I didn't even know he was back in New York yet. And then I heard it on the radio this morning."

"How long had you worked for him?"

"A little over three months. He was just out of the army

and he had some cash and these contacts so he set up an importing company."

"Then you didn't know him well." The comment was casual.

"Well?" The blond woman shrugged. "You know how it is, Lieutenant. We were both young and unattached; at least, I was unattached." She looked at Janice without embarrassment. "I didn't know about you. He never said a word about getting married. You needn't mind too much, Mrs. Maxwell. It was just one of those things. You shouldn't grudge me that. He never asked me to marry him. But then," she added philosophically, "he could get a lot like me. I'm a good pal and what a mistake that is!"

The lieutenant was obviously disturbed by these revelations and he looked warily at Jance, afraid of an outbreak of rage or grief or jealousy, but she was apparently unmoved by what she had heard. In relief he picked up the engagement pad he had placed before him.

"I see there were no appointments for Friday."

"Bob didn't intend to be back by then," Mrs. Jensen said, and it gave Janice a queer shock to hear the woman's use of his name. "He'd gone to this convention in Atlantic City that I'd set up for him on Monday, and he expected to be gone until next Monday."

"But you couldn't have made his reservation on Monday," Janice intervened. "He didn't know about the convention until Wednesday morning."

"It was Monday," Mrs. Jensen said flatly. "I wrote a letter and sent a check for his reservation. I can show you the carbon."

Janice looked down at her hands and forced them to lie quiet on her lap, forced her face to be impassive.

The lieutenant flipped pages. "Do you know the address of Mr. Maxwell's brother in Brazil?"

"Bob's address book should be in the left-hand top drawer of his desk. That's where he always kept it."

The lieutenant looked through the papers he had gathered up from the desk and picked out a battered address book, which looked as though it had, literally, gone through the war.

"Here it is, just the name Bruce and a street address in Rio. Can you put through that call for me, Mrs. Jensen?"

She wrote down the address. "I'll try, but you can really get balled up on those foreign calls. It may take a while."

The lieutenant nodded, turned back to the calendar, his expression more and more grim. Scrawled under Wednesday's date was the notation: "Janice—City Hall—twelve-thirty sharp. Don't forget ring." It was hardly the sort of entry made by an enraptured bridegroom.

Janice's phone number represented only one of the women listed, among whom he was not surprised to find the name of the typist.

With few exceptions the men listed had Chinese names. A queer setup altogether, a very queer setup. It looked as though the widow might be well out of it. He turned back to the calendar. On Tuesday there was the entry: "Two o'clock. Jade would look well with red." He looked at Janice's smooth brown hair. Looked down.

"Know any redheads, Mrs. Maxwell?"

She blinked in surprise. "No. I don't think so."

She might as well have it straight between the eyes. Sometimes that was the easiest way. "There's an entry here for Tuesday: 'Two o'clock. Jade would look well with red.' "

With a kind of jolt Janice recalled the bronze hairpins in her bedroom, in her bed, when she had returned home on Tuesday. But surely Bob would not have brought a woman there. He could not have done a thing like that on the day before his marriage. Or could he?

Apparently she had known nothing about the man she had married. He had lied to her about the convention in Atlantic City. He had lied about his background and his family. He had pretended chagrin at discovering she had more money than he. He had lied about the call he had received at the Gotham. Instead of going to the Brazilian consulate, he had gone to a midtown hotel.

She waited while Mrs. Jensen put through the call to

Brazil and the lieutenant withdrew to Bob's cubicle where he examined his files. There seemed to be something interesting, because he stored them carefully in a briefcase and gave her a formal receipt.

"We'll have to have an expert go over them. Your husband seems to have acquired some fairly extensive contacts among Chinese traders."

"Take whatever you need," Janice said listlessly.

And then Mrs. Jensen signaled the lieutenant, who picked up the telephone on Bob's desk. The call went on for a long time. When he had finished, he came to pull up a chair beside Janice.

"That was your brother-in-law. He admitted that he had always suspected that his divorce had been rigged, but he has no complaints because his second marriage suits him fine. He was considerably shocked by his brother's murder and he has no explanation to offer. He doesn't know of any enemies his brother might have had. In fact, he doesn't know any of his recent friends or business associates. Mr. Maxwell had told him only that he had a good setup and it was likely to get better.

"The last letter said that he intended to marry you as soon as possible because there was the risk of a hitch. He didn't indicate what that might be. Bruce said he hadn't a clue, but he was sorry the marriage hadn't worked out. It sounded to him as though Bob might have been onto a good thing."

Janice flushed hotly and then she said, "Yes, I am beginning to be aware of that, Lieutenant."

"I'm afraid your husband was a bad lot, Mrs. Maxwell, but that doesn't alter the fact that he was murdered. It's our job to find out who killed him."

"How can you do that with nothing to go on?"

"If you don't need me any longer," Mrs. Jensen said, "I'd like to pick up my little girl. This woman who looks after her charges double for overtime."

"Just one thing more. Where were you, Mrs. Jensen, yesterday between, say, one and four?"

"Well, Bob was away and two of my clients were doing

house-to-house canvassing, and the other one wanted me to work last night and this morning typing a price estimate. So I took off the afternoon to shop for Karen's birthday. It seemed to be all right." She sat down limply. "But it wasn't all right, was it?"

"We don't know that yet, do we? Yes, you can go. Please leave this wire open, as we may need it. And don't leave town, Mrs. Jensen."

"Where do you think I could go, Mister?"

"Wait," Janice said. "At least let me pay for the overtime. I'm responsible for keeping you here so long."

Mrs. Jensen hesitated and then shrugged. "Okay, why not?" She took the twenty-dollar bill Janice handed her and glanced at it. "Well, thanks." She rang for the elevator.

"She needs someone to help her," Janice said, troubled.

"So do you," the lieutenant told her dryly. "Do you pick up all the lame ducks?"

"Not really. There's nothing more for me to do here, is there?"

"You say you didn't know any of your husband's friends?"

"Only Hal Streichen, who introduced us."

"Who is he?"

"I've known him for years. He must be fairly well-to-do because he doesn't work at anything. He spends practically all his weekends at the inn, where he has a suite of rooms. Bob was his guest not long ago."

"How can we reach this Mr. Streichen?"

"Right now he is undoubtedly at the inn."

The lieutenant dialed the number Janice gave him. Mr. Streichen was not in his room. They were paging him in the bar, the clubroom, out of doors at the pool and on the tennis courts. Of course if he was on the lake, it might take some time to reach him.

While he waited, the lieutenant flipped through the address book and now and then took a quick, puzzled look at Janice, who sat unmoving, her hands lying quiet on her lap, her face expressionless. By how much effort of will, he wondered, was she able to maintain that control and how long could she do it? What was behind her unrevealing face? She had had a series of terrific shocks and taken them well. Too well?

"Mr. Streichen? . . . This is Lieutenant Carrigan of the New York Police. Homicide . . . No, no kidding. I am calling about the death, what may prove to be the murder, of your friend Robert Maxwell." He listened patiently. "There are just a few questions, Mr. Streichen. I understand that Mrs. Maxwell and her husband met through you . . . Yes, Miss Edwards married him on Wednesday . . . Just a casual acquaintance . . . Paying a debt . . . Well, that's all for now . . . Sorry, but I'm afraid that Mrs. Maxwell will have to know."

Janice took a long breath. "What is it now? Don't hold back, Lieutenant. Like Shakespeare, 'but in the onset come.' I might as well have it all at once. Let's get it over with."

He nodded. "Mr. Streichen says his father left him a few charge accounts, within strict limits, a room and meals at a New York apartment hotel, and a suite of rooms and expenses at Inspiration Lake, but only a hundred dollars a month in cash for life. Mr. Streichen feels aggrieved because his father indicated that he drank too much and gambled too much and in general was not reliable. As a result, he seems to feel that he was unfairly treated and that anything he does is justified." He gave Janice an uneasy look and she braced herself. Whatever was coming she was going to hate.

"Well, Streichen got into a poker game with a few returning service men who were geared for a big night. He not only lost his whole month's spending money but he had to give IOUs for the next few months, leaving him stranded. The big winner was Maxwell, who laughed and said that Streichen could call it quits if he introduced him to a rich, unattached girl and anything came of it. The other day Streichen got back his IOUs without comment."

"I see." After a moment Janice began to laugh.

Lieutenant Carrigan watched her narrowly, waiting for any sign of collapse. "Well, we are beginning to get places, at least to the point where we can eliminate a lot of red herrings. We know the call Maxwell got did not come from Brazil. Now who would have known where he could be reached at that particular time?"

"I never thought of that! I remember Bob was surprised and said that nobody knew he was to be there."

"And now that you do think of it?"

Janice frowned in perplexity. "No one could know that we were lunching at the Gotham except my boss and an author of his who saw us there."

"Your boss?" Carrigan asked.

Janice explained.

"Fitzgerald. Fitz? Is he the one who sent you the flowers and the note?"

"Yes."

"Great friend of yours?"

"A good friend though I haven't known him very long."

"Any personal interest?"

"Good heavens, no!"

"So your marriage would not alter your relations with him in any way?"

"No, I planned to go on working."

"Any financial transactions?"

"I don't understand. Just my salary, of course. A hundred a week."

Recalling the penthouse, Carrigan said, "Just a token salary."

"Well, yes, but I didn't need the money and he can't afford to pay more. It's hard getting started with a new house. He was saying not long ago that he might have to sell out; he'd had an offer, but I urged him not to. I have him down in my will for a hundred thousand for the firm and I told him he can have it now if he likes."

The lieutenant was watching her closely. Her hands were clenching and unclenching. Her defenses were beginning to crack.

"Can't you go to a friend tonight? Surely you don't want to return to that big empty apartment. And you may have to run the gauntlet of the press again."

"I don't think it matters," Janice said listlessly. "What are you planning to do next?"

"I think I'll have a little talk with Mr. Fitzgerald, Mrs. Maxwell."

"Please," she said, her control breaking, "please don't call me that. It's not as though I was ever really his wife."

NINE

FITZ INTERRUPTED Janice's agitated words, which stumbled over each other. "Stop. Take a few long breaths and then begin again. I can't make out a thing you are saying. You are wheezing like an overage steam engine."

Janice, who had rushed to telephone him as soon as she returned home, found herself laughing.

"That's better," he said encouragingly.

"I was anxious to get hold of you before the police do. Oh, Fitz, I'm afraid I've got you into the most awful jam."

"Actually, I am the one who blundered. I should have had more sense than to send you those roses with such a fervent note, which, I gather, the police read."

"Oh, dear, you mean they've been to see you already," she exclaimed in dismay.

"Pull yourself together, girl. No harm has been done."

"But what did they ask you?"

"They wanted to know," he said with maddening calm, "whether I was aware that you had made me a legatee in your will, and I admitted that I did know it. They then were interested in checking my financial situation, and I told them where they could find out and said I hoped they would be able to understand it better than I do."

"Oh, don't joke, Fitz! It's no joking matter."

"And then—and please don't keep interrupting me; it

breaks my chain of thought—they wanted to know how long you had worked for me, how well I knew you, and whether I had been informed in advance of your marriage to Maxwell."

"Is that all?" she said in relief.

"Not quite all." He sounded amused. "They confirmed my knowledge that Mr. Maxwell lunched at the Gotham on Friday. They also inquired into my movements on Friday afternoon."

He cut short her exclamation of horror. "I'm glad you called me, Janice. I tried to get you but you aren't answering your phone, which is understandable, and your apartment switchboard refused to put me through. What I wanted to say is this: Get out of that place and go up to your lake until you can adjust a bit to what has happened. Dave is there, you know, and he'll be at your service. Happy to be. The police certainly won't have any objection to your going there, as long as they can reach you, and right now, while they have a suspicious eye on me, perhaps it would be better for you to stay away from the office. It would be unrestful to have them dropping in at all hours to see what we are up to."

"But that's outrageous! What on earth could make them think that you would kill Bob?"

"Well, for one thing, I might be afraid that you would change your will and, with his influence or without it, include me out."

"Ridiculous."

"And the second reason, of course," Fitz went on in his calm voice, "is the conviction of the police that I might want to eliminate Maxwell in order to marry you myself."

"Oh!" It was less an exclamation than the kind of sound a person makes when he has taken a sudden punch that knocks the breath out of him. "Of all the—as though you had ever—"

"I know. Slow on the uptake, wasn't I? But I thought you were still finding yourself. I didn't realize that you were ready—Oh, skip it."

"Fitz?" It was a shaken question.

"Get on up to Inspiration Lake," he said briskly, and she thought that she must have been mistaken about the warm inflection in his voice.

"You are being very considerate," she told him.

"Don't you believe it. I'm playing the filthiest possible trick on you, but it's my conviction that in some cases it's a question of kill or cure, and I don't want the shadow of Robert Maxwell between—oh, hell, get going, Janice. Anything I can do—write or call or just snap your fingers —but you know that." He hung up abruptly.

Janice looked at the silent telephone as though expecting it to answer her startled question and then she shook herself impatiently and arranged for a plane to Inspiration Lake, telephoned Bertie to pick her up at the airport, and called the police to inform them of her plans. She ordered a taxi, tied a scarf around her head; packed what cosmetics and clothes she needed in a pillow slip, and came out of the areaway, ignoring the patient newsmen. Then at the curb she jumped so quickly into the waiting cab that she could hear the startled exclamation of a frustrated cameraman as she was driven off.

She was the only passenger on the small plane and she sat staring into the night, trying to bring some order into her chaotic thoughts, to grasp what had happened. A few things were clear. On all counts she had been wrong about Bob Maxwell. He had married her in a rush because he had been afraid of some obstacle to the wedding. He had known that she would be a pushover. Hal Streichen had known that, too. Janice the wallflower, so unaccustomed to masculine attentions that she was swept off her feet by the first man to declare he loved her. But that was not quite true. There had been Thomas.

She shifted restlessly on the seat. Bob might have been the only man in her life, but there was no question about the women in his. Could one of them have hated him enough to kill him? His sister-in-law, whose marriage he had broken up? The typist who had been his mistress? The woman who had left bronze hairpins in Janice's bedroom?

None of this mattered any longer. What mattered was

that Bob had been jubilant when he returned from Atlantic City and then something had gone wrong. The telephone call at the Gotham had wiped away his triumph and he had left her, prepared to some extent, to meet his murderer. That was all that could account for the disguise.

And that brought her to Fitz, who had set the pattern of the daily lunches at the Gotham, and who had known that Bob was there. Fitz had been questioned by the police because of the bequest in her will, the roses he had sent her, and what he had referred to as his fervent message. Anyone would think, from the way he had spoken on the telephone, that he loved her, that he had only waited to tell her so until he believed her to be ready.

There I go again, Janice warned herself, ready to believe a man who claims to love me. But Fitz? True, he had stormed out of the office on Friday without explanation and after an uncharacteristic outburst of temper, a thing he had never done before. He had made some bitter comment about not keeping the bridegroom waiting. But there was no escaping the fact that Fitz and Dave McClintock were the only people who knew Bob would be at the Gotham.

Bertie was waiting with the station wagon. This time, subdued and shocked, he took her suitcase without a word and settled her in the back of the car. When he opened the door for her at Peaceful Haven, he said, "My wife was afraid you wouldn't bother with dinner, so she set out a little supper for you, which she hopes you will try to eat."

"That was thoughtful of her."

"You'll be here for a while?"

"I'll have to return to New York on Tuesday for the inquest. The funeral service will be on Wednesday. After that, I don't know."

"Mrs. Maxwell—"

"I think I'll go on being Miss Edwards. Good night."

The little supper Mrs. Bertie had prepared consisted of a thermos of hot crab bisque, small sandwiches of chicken and ham and cucumber, and a half bottle of white wine chilling in a bucket of ice. There was a note: "Please try to eat it all to keep up your strength. I kept a list of calls. Mary Bertie."

After pouring a glass of the chilled white wine and sipping it, Janice discovered that she was famished. While she drank the soup and nibbled at sandwiches, she looked over the sheaf of telephone messages:

"Tell Mrs. Maxwell that Hal Streichen called and said he can explain everything. That policeman couldn't take a joke."

"Vladimir Strunski called to express his sympathy and say he is having a few friends next weekend and hopes very much that you will join them. Nothing to make you feel awkward while you are in mourning, and there will be some great music-making, as Golschmann is coming."

"A Mr. David McClintock called to say he'd be happy to be of any service. Any use at all. He said to tell you that Fitz had been in touch with him."

"Mrs. Nichols telephoned and said that you are to call *at once*."

"Mr. Thomas Nichols called four times. He did not leave a message. Do not call him; he will call you."

It was only after she had gone to bed, just on the verge of sleep, that Janice found herself wondering idly where Thomas had been on Friday afternoon.

II

It was nearly noon when a tap on the door was followed by Mrs. Bertie carrying a breakfast tray.

"I'm that sorry to be disturbing you, Mrs.—uh—Miss Edwards, knowing how you need your rest. I wouldn't call you for anything else, though that phone has rung all morning, but the last call was from a New York policeman. I said I wouldn't have you talking until you'd had your breakfast, but I did promise to wake you up right away, which I would a whole lot rather not have done."

"That's all right. And thank you for the supper you left last night. I ate all of it."

Mrs. Bertie beamed. "And I was mighty pleased to see you had."

"What did the policeman want? Did he tell you?"

"He just said there were some new developments. He didn't say what." There was avid curiosity in the woman's face, but she asked no questions. She would never, Janice realized gratefully, ask questions. The Berties were beyond price.

When she had finished breakfast and dressed in slacks and a soft yellow shirt, she took a green sweater and, after a glance at herself, went downstairs. It occurred to her that for a woman who had been widowed without ever having been a wife, whose husband had died horribly and mysteriously and who had learned through a series of shocking revelations that he was a thoroughly bad actor, she looked remarkably well. Her eyes were clear, her skin glowed. The long sleep and Mrs. Bertie's superlative food had performed miracles. And perhaps, she admitted honestly to herself, the revelations about Bob's real character and what she now knew to be the truth of his regard for her, made it impossible to suffer any genuine grief. Shocked and horrified and bewildered. Above all, she was humiliated as a woman. But she was not grief-stricken and she was resolved not to pretend that she was, simply out of respect for the conventions. Emotional dishonesty was the worst kind and the hardest to avoid if one cared much about the opinion of one's fellows.

Lieutenant Carrigan sounded cheerful when she got in touch with him. "Sorry to disturb you, Miss Edwards. I expect you needed your rest."

"I did, but I'm fine now."

"Good. You sound that way. Well, I've got some news for you."

"You know who killed Bob!" She didn't know whether she was relieved or sorry.

"No, and I must admit that's as big a puzzle now as it has been all along. What we've got is a totally new development. We had a man check on your husband's business associates, the men he is dealing with in this importing business of his—and how that was being handled defeats me. Every one of his contacts checks back to a Mainland source."

"Mainland?" Janice was bewildered.

"In some way Maxwell acquired close ties with a group of businessmen in Communist China. The deal appears to be worked from Hong Kong, but actually—"

"I don't understand at all, Lieutenant. Communist China? You mean that while he was in the army Bob was in communication with the Communists? But that would make him a traitor, wouldn't it?"

"Your guess is as good as ours, ma'am. All we know for sure is that, in one way or another—and it's got to be while he was in Vietnam—he got a line on handling goods smuggled out of Hong Kong and shipped over to him. We've found a warehouse with a lot of jade and bales of silk and curios and some silk scrolls that an expert tells me are museum pieces. Frankly, the whole situation stinks."

Janice had no comment to make.

"You know," the lieutenant went on, "this is a funny thing," though he did not sound as though he thought it was funny. "When the body was picked up outside the hotel, it looked easy. Then we discovered the disguise. Oh, and by the way, we found that a reservation was made on Monday for the convention at Atlantic City, as Mrs. Jensen told us, and a check sent to pay for the room. All according to Hoyle. But he never showed up. The people who attended the convention are strictly legitimate, men of good standing, and none of them ever heard of Maxwell or Far East Imports. We had a man interview a lot of them, because the final banquet was held last night and most of them stayed on for that.

"So that leaves us with an alibi carefully prepared in advance, and we haven't a clue as to why he needed it, what he was actually doing. When he called you on Friday to say he was leaving Atlantic City, God knows where he really was. I have a hunch he was right here in New York.

"Now, aside from what seems to be an extremely shady

business setup, we find that he had aroused the resentment of his sister-in-law who, if you'll pardon the expression, hated his guts and has no alibi for the time when he was killed. And that might apply to Mrs. Jensen as well; she certainly wasn't prepared to hear that he was married. And there were other women, Miss Edwards. We are checking them out as fast as we can, of course. And on top of all that we find out that your employer, Gamaliel Fitzgerald, not only stood to gain by your will—"

"I might point out, Lieutenant," and there was an edge on Janice's voice, "that it was my husband who was killed —not I."

"I know, but people usually change their wills when they marry, and this guy was obviously upset by your marriage. Knocked off his feet, I'd say. He was careful about what he said to us, weighing his words, trying not to give anything away, but any fool could see he had no use at all for Maxwell and thought you were well out of it. And he hasn't an alibi for Friday afternoon that is worth a damn."

"Oh, no!" Janice exclaimed in distress.

"He claims that he spent the afternoon in the cardroom at the Forty-second Street Branch of the New York Public Library, looking up source material for an author."

"Not Fitz," Janice said. "It couldn't be Fitz."

"Well, I promised to report. That's today's installment of this thrilling real-life drama. Sorry, I didn't mean to sound smart."

"Never mind. What are you going to do now?"

"We're checking back on every day Maxwell spent in the service. If, as appears, he had Communist contacts, he must have made them there. Must have. I'll keep in touch, Miss Edwards. You understand that you are to attend the inquest on Tuesday? You'll be called upon to testify about that telephone call at the Gotham. Nothing to it. They'll adjourn."

Janice set down the telephone and, having assured Mrs. Bertie that, after so late a breakfast, she required no lunch, she slipped on her sweater and went out to walk through the woods, strolling aimlessly, enjoying the deep carpet of pine needles under her feet, the scent of fir and balsam in the air.

She skirted the cottages until she caught sight of Helen Peters hanging clothes on a rack. When she heard Janice's approach, she looked at the girl keenly and then expelled a little sigh of relief.

"I was afraid—"

Janice assured her that she was all right. A terrible thing, of course, a horrible shock. But not a tragedy. "I've learned too much about Bob for it to matter as it might have, so, please, Helen—"

"I'm not going to say a word except about Grace Nichols. Keep away from her or you'll be married to Lou yet. I don't believe she's really taken in the fact of your marriage to another man."

"How is Lou?"

"You can't prove anything by me. Of course we have all inquired and offered our services. I caught only one glimpse of him, strolling through the woods and, except that he is much too thin, he looked all right to me, perfectly cheerful, smiling to himself. But Grace came rushing out after him and took him back to the cottage. She claims that someone has been prowling around the place and spying on him, which is absurd. She guards him like a dog with a bone. And poor Thomas! He looks as though he had aged in the past few weeks. I suppose he'll be expected to wait hand and foot on the returned hero. There seems to be no justice for people like Thomas, does there?"

When Janice made no reply, Helen said rather nervously, "I'm so relieved that Mr. Maxwell's death has not been the great tragedy I feared. There was gossip at the time he was up here with Hal Streichen that Sonia latched onto him and that they danced together both nights he was here."

"Sonia?" In a different tone Janice repeated, enlightened, "Sonia! Oh, of course. Only it never occurred to me."

"Well, it doesn't mean anything. It never does with Sonia. Right now she is flaunting a gorgeous jade ring which she claims is a family heirloom she has just unearthed. Poor Vladimir is trying to look as though he believed it, but he's not being very convincing. In some ways Sonia really is a fool. She is sitting pretty, with a position such as few men could give her, surrounded by a circle of brilliant people, and heaven knows Vladimir is willing to leave her free enough. But he isn't the kind of man who will be content to be made a fool of, not in public, at any rate. He's too vain for that. One of these days he is going to stab her or do something equally drastic."

Struck by a new notion, Janice said, "I wonder—do you know whether Sonia went to New York last week?"

"She went twice; once with Grace Nichols on Tuesday to help her buy some civilian clothes for Lou, and both the Strunskis went in on Friday. In fact, the whole colony went except for me; even Jake, who took that painting you liked to select a proper frame for it. That is, if you still want it. There is no obligation, you know."

"I certainly want it."

"Oh, Lord! Well, it's too late to duck." Helen raised her voice. "Good afternoon, Grace. Wonderful day, isn't it?"

Grace Nichols trudged around the hedge and looked at the laundry rack. "It will never dry in the shade. Move it out in the sun, Helen. I declare, you're as impractical as Jake." She turned to Janice. "I was looking for you. I couldn't believe my ears when I heard that you had married after being engaged to Lou all this time. Well, of course, it's all right now."

Even Helen Peters, accustomed to Mrs. Nichols as she was, gaped at this comment.

"Come along and see Lou. From now on it's your rightful job to take care of him."

TEN

FEET POUNDED along the path. As soon as Thomas caught sight of the three women, he dropped to a walk and tried to control his rapid breathing. As he looked at Janice, he turned a dark red and then his color faded.

"Hello, Janice. I wanted—we're all so shocked and grieved about your tragedy." He mopped his head with a shaking hand, and Helen Peters gave him a queer, searching look.

"Thank you, Thomas, but I'd be awfully grateful if no one attempted to discuss it with me. That would be the kindest thing."

"Yes, of course. Whatever you say. Mother," and he took her arm, "I was looking for you."

"I came over to get Janice."

"Yes, well—the stuff you have in the oven is burning." As Grace started to protest, Thomas's hand tightened on her arm. She yielded reluctantly to the insistent pressure and let him take her away.

"Something was burning," Helen Peters said. "Of all the lame excuses I ever heard! Poor Thomas. I think Jake is right when he says that someday Thomas is going to crack up. No man can be expected to take what he does. But for once he seems to have the upper hand on Grace. She went along meekly enough. And I got the impression

—dear heaven, don't tell me that Thomas wants to marry you! That would really put the lid on it. If I were you, I'd head for the North Pole and stay there until the dust settles."

"It's not that bad." Janice was eager to get away from the subject of Thomas. One look had been enough to tell her the extent of the shock he had sustained by her marriage. Belatedly she recalled his grim comment that if Lou married her he would kill him, and she had married Bob instead. But Thomas couldn't have known. Anyhow, people made empty threats like that all the time, and they didn't mean a thing.

"When am I going to see my picture?" she said.

"Come in. Jake is really satisfied for once, though he won't admit it. And he's on the right track at last. He's doing a lovely thing now, a pool—well, actually, it's a puddle left by the rain, but somehow you know the rain has just stopped. I don't know why I like it so much. Anyhow, Jake won't mind you coming in while it's unfinished."

Jake, as she might have known, did not refer to her marriage and bereavement. He glanced casually over his shoulder as she came into the studio, nodded, and continued making up his palette. Janice went straight to the long canvas propped against the wall in a simple, dark frame.

"Oh, Jake, I'm going to love this more and more. It's really a painting to live with. I'm going to hang it in my apartment on the wall across from the windows where it will get a wonderful light. And when you hold your one-man show on Fifty-seventh Street, I'll lend it to you."

"Fifty-seventh Street," he scoffed, but his eyes brightened.

"I'll have Bertie pick it up at your convenience, and perhaps you'll advise him on the best way to ship it."

He nodded. "Wasn't that our patient Thomas I heard out there?" He stood back to look at his canvas.

"Yes, he came to get his mother."

"Uh-huh. If you'll take advice from an old man, stay away from the whole Nichols tribe. And perhaps the easiest thing for you to do would be to inform Mrs. Nichols that, as there is no longer a creative worker in the family, you will have to ask them to vacate the cottage."

"Jake! I couldn't. Not possibly."

"Then have your lawyers do it. Don't be soft-hearted about this. Believe me, I'm talking good hard sense, Janice. You'd be completely justified, you know. Ransome never meant this place to be used by people who weren't working in the arts."

"I know, but—"

"Jake is right," Helen put in. "They are imposing on you; they have no right here; and, besides, they are mak- your life miserable."

"If you like," Jake offered, "I'll do it for you after you go back to the city. It will be all over before you return."

"You are incredibly kind, but I couldn't; I simply couldn't. It would be too cruel."

"Well, when you change your mind and come to your senses, I'll handle it for you."

Impulsively Janice kissed his cheek. "I love you both."

"Be strange if you didn't," he said blandly, and she laughed.

II

Underfoot she felt the soft spongy yielding of a thick bed of pine needles on the path. She walked through dappled woods, the sun dazzling bright at moments and then hidden by a curtain of trees. As she walked, she was thinking of Jake's alluring offer to rid her of the Nichols family, a prospect as delightful as it was impossible.

Overhead a bird sang shrilly and then she was aware of the sounds from the Strunski cottage. Vladimir was playing Debussy, iridescent, elusive, the music dripping from his fingers like drops of water. She was aware, because he had told her so with some severity, that Debussy had a spine and a shape, but to her the music was as bodiless as soap bubbles or smoke dissolving in air.

She paused, propping herself against a tree, listening. There was a pause and then he played some muscular Brahms; another pause, as though searching for something to fit his mood, and then came some crisp Scarlatti. Of late years Vladimir Strunski had made few concert appearances except in his own concerto, but his technique seemed as solid and clean as ever.

In the middle of the Scarlatti he broke off and appeared in the door of his studio. "Janice! I just saw you standing out there. Do come in."

"Oh, I—"

As though aware of the reason for her reluctance, he said casually, "Sonia is at the inn getting in some tennis with Hal Streichen. I'm in a mood to play today and I always like an audience. So if you'd care to listen, come along."

Vladimir Strunski was a small man, spare, with white hair and yellowish eyes set in pouches so that they resembled poached eggs, and he looked every day of his seventy years. His Russian accent was heavy, particularly when he was excited, and he was often excited. Perhaps because he was so small, not over five-foot-four, his bearing was stately and his movements deliberate, and he talked like a man accustomed to being listened to. He was vain, cynical, disillusioned, and apt to attitudinize. Only when he was playing or composing was he completely honest. He was a scrupulous artist.

Janice took a chair in the little studio and Strunski immediately began to play, taking the Scarlatti from the beginning. Then he said, without turning around, "What would you like to hear?"

"Would you be disgusted if I ask for some Chopin?"

"Disgusted? Why? What a musical snob you must take me for. There is beautiful music in Chopin." He plunged into one of the dizzying études. When he had finished, he said, while his hands sketched soundless arpeggios over the keyboard, "Did you get my message about the party next weekend?"

"Yes, but I'm afraid it will be impossible for me to come."

"There will be some great music, which is good for the soul. You won't need to talk to anyone if you prefer it that way. There will be some trios as well as Golschmann at the piano, probably the 'Archduke.' I'm inviting a number of interesting people to the inn. This is to be my last big party for the season and I want it to be a success."

"Your parties are always successes, aren't they?"

"That's because of Sonia, who has a flair for entertaining. She should have married someone like the French Rothschild so as to have fuller scope for her social talents."

"Oh, no, there's no one who would have suited her more than you." As the musician laughed, Janice said earnestly, "But it's true, you know. Sonia thrives in the company of creative people. Helen was pointing that out not long ago; Sonia engenders creative ideas in others."

"That is so," Strunski said thoughtfully, "but she doesn't limit her—enthusiasm—to creative men." He turned around to meet her eyes. When he turned back, he played the Chopin third étude softly, with a singing tone. By the time he had finished, he had forgotten her presence and he tackled the Revolutionary étude, each disciplined note of the left hand taken at a snail's pace. Aware that she was forgotten, Janice went quietly out of the studio.

Helen had been right then in saying that Strunski was jealous of his wife's amorous activities, but it seemed extreme to imagine that he would ever be stirred to violence. Certainly he would not kill anyone because of one of Sonia's fleeting infidelities. Anyhow, he was old and so small he could never have coped with Bob, young and big and at the peak of his strength.

Janice trudged on through the woods, away from the sound of Vladimir's piano. She saw a fox stand as still as a statue and then run for cover. People talked enviously about the freedom of wildlife, but there was one freedom no wild animal could ever attain—freedom from fear.

She heard a woman's soft, provocative laughter, and saw Sonia in a short white tennis dress, which was unkind to her plump legs, emerge from the cottage Dave McClintock had taken. He was standing behind her in the doorway.

"Are you sure you can manage" she was asking. "I have nothing to do and I'd be glad to wait until it has had time to bake."

"Thanks, but I can manage beautifully. I'm becoming quite a cook. You have been most kind."

"It was my pleasure. Oh, by the way, Vladimir is giving a party next weekend, cocktails at six, dinner at seven, music later. Interesting people. You'll enjoy it."

"I really came up here to work, you know."

"Foolish boy! All work and no play."

"But I'm a very dull boy."

She patted his cheek with a scented hand on which Janice saw a jade ring, and started down the path. As she caught sight of Janice, she came to an abrupt halt. Slowly, inexorably, a flood of color washed over her face and down her throat.

Janice was sure now that the bronze hairpins had been Sonia's and that, impossibly, she had been in the penthouse with Bob on Tuesday afternoon.

"Oh, Janice, my dear, we were all so shocked to hear—"

How was one supposed to greet the woman who had slept in her bed with her fiancé the day before her wedding? Janice looked in appeal at Dave, who said promptly, "How kind of you to come so soon! I hadn't dared to hope that you would. If you can stop now, it won't take long to settle everything."

"Of course I can," Janice said with such alacrity that Sonia gave her a swift, speculative look before she went away with her swaying walk.

Dave stood back to let Janice enter the cottage and then closed the door. "I had no idea," he commented, "of the hazards attached to living up here." Then the grin faded and he pulled out a chair for her. "I thought you might want to get rid of her."

"I did. And, by the way, her husband assumes that she is playing tennis at the inn."

"Does he indeed? Well, not even Othello could read

anything clandestine into her teaching me how to prepare a casserole."

"How is the cottage?"

"It's perfect. The whole setup—with the exception of sinuous Sonia, and I can cope with her—is fabulous. And, to top it all, Fitz likes the beginning I have made on the book."

No one, she thought, could sound more delighted; no one could look less so. He went to stand at the window with his back to her.

"Mrs Maxwell," he began abruptly.

"Miss Edwards, or why not Janice? But, please, not Mrs. Maxwell."

"I'm glad," he said, responding to her tone rather than to the words; "that makes it easier. I thought, or rather Fitz thought, you ought to know the truth, but I hate like hell having to tell you."

"Is it something about Bob?"

He nodded without turning around.

"Then you may as well tell me. I've learned so much since he died, discovered what sort of man he was; got an insight into what a credulous, gullible fool I have been, that, at this point, nothing would make any difference."

"This will make a difference." Dave came to pull out a chair facing her. "Do you remember when we lunched together that day I told you of the man in our prison camp who betrayed a prisoner attempting to escape and as a result was tortured?"

Janice nodded and then her eyes widened. "Bob?" She shaped the word with her lips without any sound coming out.

"Yes. I recognized him at once when Fitz and I passed your table, and I never wanted anything more in my life than I wanted to expose him then and there. But Fitz had told me that you had just married him and you had done so much for me, arranging all this," and he indicated the cottage. "I didn't know what to do. But one thing I couldn't do was to stand there and shake hands with the man."

"You told Fitz?"

"Of course."

"When?"

"Oh, at once. We were still talking about it when you came back to the office."

"Bob," she said wonderingly. "Bob did that."

"I can tell you this, Mrs.—Janice. He deserved what he got."

"No one has a right to appoint himself executioner."

"You think not?"

After a moment Janice said, "I remember you told me that if you could lay hands on him you would kill him."

"Well, I didn't, if that is what is worrying you." His prompt denial was oddly unconvincing.

"But his murderer paged him at the Gotham and only you and Fitz knew of his presence there. And Fitz had no motive for killing him."

Dave started to speak, closed his lips firmly. At last he said, "Well, I promised Fitz I would tell you the truth about your husband. If you think I killed him, can you see any good reason why I would carefully explain to you just how strong a motive I had? I may be a fool, but not a damned fool."

"So that is what Fitz meant about playing a filthy trick on me. Kill or cure, he said."

Dave made no comment.

"I suppose, if it should be necessary, you could tell the police just how you spent Friday afternoon."

As he became aware of her attitude, his own changed. The friendliness faded. He spoke with the detachment of a man making a report: "I did some shopping at Abercrombie's; I ordered a supply of typewriter ribbons and paper, and the tools of my trade: dictionary, thesaurus, Bartlett's *Familiar Quotations,* a one-volume Shakespeare, Fowler's *Modern English Usage.* I also got a shave and a haircut." He cocked an eyebrow. "Not good enough? Sorry, but that's the best I can come up with."

She did not respond to his light tone, his deliberately light tone. "Dave, who was on the plane when you came back Friday afternoon?"

His eyes narrowed. He did not look so pleasant now and not at all amused. "Trying to test my story? I had, as you can see for yourself, plenty of time to push Maxwell out of a window and still make the five o'clock plane."

She made a gesture of impatience. "I really want to know."

"The whole colony," he told her. "I haven't met them all, but I know who they are." He checked them off on his fingers. "Both the Strunskis, Mr. Peters, Mrs. Nichols and her son Thomas. Oh, and the inn guests, of course. The only one of those I've met is Maxwell's friend, Hal Streichen."

"I'd forgotten Hal," Janice admitted.

"He's the kind of guy people are bound to forget," Dave said indifferently. "The perennial playboy. How does he manage to support this life of indolence?"

"I'm beginning to wonder," Janice said slowly. She added in a tone of surprise, "I don't understand how Grace Nichols managed to leave her son long enough to go to New York twice in a week. She rarely leaves the lake. And where Lou is concerned, she is ridiculous. She is now claiming, I understand, that someone has been prowling around the cottage, spying on him. She's really getting to the point where she imagines things."

"Well, she didn't imagine that," Dave said unexpectedly. "There was someone hanging around on Thursday. I work only in the mornings, and in the afternoons I go for a walk or a swim. I saw this guy looking in the window of the Nichols cottage. I thought it was just someone from the inn out for a stroll and wanting to see how those queer creatures, artists, live."

"Could it have been a tramp? We've never had any."

"Unlikely. He was well dressed. Middle-aged, I'd say. Quite bald and one of those old-fashioned goatees and a kind of lumpy face. Reminded me of Brando in *The Godfather*."

"Perhaps for the same reason." Janice said queerly.

"What do you mean?"

"Disguise. Make-up. That's the way Bob looked when I saw him in the morgue."

At last Dave said softly, "My God! Oh, good God! But why?"

"On Thursday he was supposed to be in Atlantic City at a convention. He had set that up as an alibi several days in advance. At least, that is what Lieutenant Carrigan believes. But why here? Why the Nichols cottage?"

"Janice!" Dave seized her wrist, shook it. "This Lou—is he usually called Welsh?"

"Not that I ever heard of."

"What's his full name?"

"Llewellyn Jones Nichols the Third."

Dave released her wrist. "I think I'll get along to the Nichols cottage. I'm going to get a look at the elusive Lou if I have to smash my way in."

Janice stared at him, her hand covering her mouth. "If Bob did that," she choked, "if it was Lou he betrayed—"

"If he did, it's easy to see why he had to know for sure whether Welsh could betray him."

"The obstacle;" Janice exclaimed. "Bob wrote his brother that there might be an obstacle to our marriage. Then he came back and he was—relaxed, triumphant."

"No time like the present. I'll be in touch." Without any further comment Dave went out, leaving Janice alone in the cottage staring after him.

She walked back to Peaceful Haven, trying to absorb and assess her new knowledge. Knowledge or speculation? Truth or fiction?

"I don't want to take any calls," she instructed Bertie, "and I don't want to see anyone. Make any excuse you like."

She shut herself in her stepfather's den, a room which she had formerly hated, as it was an arsenal of rifles, shotguns, and handguns, but with a businesslike desk and filing case. She sat at the desk, her hands clasped in front of her. Then she caught sight of the wedding ring shining on her finger. She flung open the window, pulled off the ring and hurled it as far as she could. With a feeling of liberation she returned to the desk.

The sound of raised voices caught her attention.

"Miss Edwards is not seeing anyone." Bertie was saying firmly.

There was a scuffle, heavy footsteps down the hall, and Thomas walked into the room. "You keep evading me. I've got to talk to you, Janice. I've got to."

Bertie appeared in the doorway, looking harassed.

"It's all right," Janice assured him. "Mr. Nichols has some business to discuss with me. It won't take long. Be ready to drive him back in half an hour."

Thomas gave a bark of laughter. "Last time you offered me an hour. My stock seems to be going down."

"What do you want, Thomas?"

Now that he was close to her, she was shocked by the alteration in his appearance; he looked older, haggard.

"I don't suppose I have any right to ask, but I'm just about going crazy. Why did you marry that man, Janice? Were you in love with him?"

She swallowed her anger and impatience and responded to the anguish in his face. "I don't know, Thomas," she said honestly. "Certainly I thought I did."

"The news of your marriage came as a shock to us all."

"With your mother acting as though I belonged to Lou, what else could we do?" Janice demanded, carrying the war into the enemy's camp.

"I know. I'm sorry about everything. You aren't planning to stay here, are you?"

"I have to go back to New York for the inquest on Tuesday and the funeral service on Wednesday. After that I don't know. I don't seem to be capable of making any plans."

"Stay in town for a while at least," Thomas said urgently. "That would be better for everyone."

For whom? Janice wondered. For me? For Thomas? For Grace? For Lou?

"How is Lou?"

"Fine," Thomas said too heartily. "Just fine. In fact,

we—he is talking of going out west before long. Big business opportunity."

"Oh, I'm glad!" Janice exclaimed in genuine relief. "But I suppose your mother won't like that."

"I might persuade her to go along." He moved around the room uneasily. He never seemed to feel quite at home anywhere; even in his own cottage he was the perpetual outsider. He put his hands in his pockets and then took them out again. "Who's this friend of yours who has come up here?"

"He's not my friend. He is a Fitzgerald author who is writing a book. That's what the colony was designed for, you know."

Thomas swallowed. "I realize that. I've been aware of it ever since Dad's suicide. We have no right to the cottage. But Mr. Ransome was willing to let Mother stay on and she had her heart set on it."

"So she could keep an eye on me."

"Well—yes."

"Does Lou know that I am here? Does he know about my marriage?"

There was a long pause and then Thomas said, "No, he doesn't know. Go away, for God's sake, Janice!" He turned on his heel and went out of the room. His heavy steps sounded down the hall and Janice heard Bertie speak, heard Thomas reply, "Thanks, but I'd rather walk."

In a few minutes Bertie came into the room to lay a piece of paper before her and go out silently. She looked at the message:

Mr. McClintock telephoned. He said he had made a positive identification. He urges you to return to New York as soon as possible."

ELEVEN

AGAIN, AS SHE boarded the plane for New York on Sunday evening, Hal Streichen took Janice away from under Thomas's nose.

"Look, I've been wanting to see you, to explain. That dumb cop couldn't take a joke."

"It wasn't," Janice told him wearily, "a very funny joke."

"But I—"

"Please sit somewhere else, Hal," she begged him. "I'm not in the mood to talk, certainly not to you." Then as she saw Thomas watching them, she capitulated. "Oh, well, stay where you are, but just don't bother me."

He gave her a sidelong look of mingled embarrassment and apology. "Whatever you say," he said with the first trace of humility she had ever seen in him, and he sank his chin on his chest and went to sleep.

Janice went back to the thoughts that had occupied her since she had received Dave's message. Lou was the man whom Bob had betrayed, who had been tortured and then thrust out of the camp to die, or at least to silence his screams, who had survived by a miracle.

It must have been an awful shock to Bob to learn that his victim had not only survived but that he was expected home, where he could implicate Bob, make his marriage impossible, and perhaps lead to his arrest and trial. An obstacle, he had said. So he had set up an elaborate alibi and had gone to Inspiration Lake in disguise to look over the situation and find out for himself how much of a threat Lou Nichols posed. He had come back to New York relaxed and triumphant. Why? That was the bewildering factor.

Suppose the recognition had been mutual. According to Helen Peters, Lou, except for being underweight, had seemed to be all right, capable of going around by himself. And he had a car. He could have driven to New York. It was an eight-hour drive, but he could have managed it and his mother and brother, knowing of his absence, would have protected him fiercely.

And God knows, Janice admitted to herself, if ever anyone might have felt justified in killing, Lou was the man. But, she checked herself, no man is justified in taking the law into his own hands. If Lou had done so, was it because of what Bob had done to him or because of Janice's marriage? Thomas had said that Lou was ignorant of her marriage, but she had not believed him. He had been too emphatic and he had warned her to stay away from the lake. Did that mean that he knew or suspected Lou's guilt and he was afraid for her or that he wanted her away for his own peace of mind?

What, she wondered, was she to tell Lieutenant Carrigan? How much of her suspicion in regard to Lou was it fair to tell the police? Lou had suffered enough.

Next morning, she made herself go into the guest room where Bob had left his things. Until then she had not touched them. She went through carefully, sorting suits—beautifully tailored suits, she observed—shirts, ties, shorts, socks, making neat piles of shoes and shaving tackle, hair tonic and lotions. There were new and unworn silk pajamas and an elaborate dressing gown. What the well-dressed bridegroom will wear, she thought, and was appalled by her own bitterness. After all, the man had died horribly.

There were some letters which, after a moment of discomfort, she opened. Never before had she read without permission letters addressed to another person. He seemed to have been on a mailing list for curios, there was a tailor's bill, a letter from a young woman that whipped color into Janice's face and which she started to destroy and then remembered that it might be evidence. There was a letter from a man identifying himself as a former army acquaintance, a letter with a curious undercurrent as though it contained a covert threat.

"Be better to meet and talk it over, don't you agree?" That, too, she put aside for Lieutenant Carrigan.

Light streaming in the window reflected on something shining. Under the edge of the bed there was a long yellow envelope, made of plastic, and containing, as she saw in surprise, $15,000 in traveler's checks, in one-hundred-dollar denominations, made out to Richard Manning.

Janice telephoned to make an appointment with the lieutenant. When he had greeted her pleasantly, she began by saying that she had gone through Robert Maxwell's effects and asked what should be done with them. He suggested that she call the Goodwill Industries. Then she handed him the letters, which, he admitted, he had read. Both the writer of erotic letters and the writer of the blackmail letter were being sought. "As though we hadn't enough suspects in this case," he said with a shake of the head.

Then she handed him the plastic envelope containing the traveler's checks.

"Where," he asked in a queer voice, "did you find this?"

"It had fallen under the edge of the bed and the sun just happened to strike it. I suppose it fell out when your men were looking through the clothes."

"I examined the clothes myself. The letters were lying in a neat little bundle on top of them. I told you, didn't I, that someone else had already searched your husband's things." He made a call and asked for a handwriting expert, "on the double." When the man appeared he gave him the traveler's checks. "Compare these with Maxwell's signature and make it fast. Well, Mrs.—Miss Edwards, anything else?"

And in the long run she told him everything she knew.

It was not for her to decide what was relevant. She told him Dave's story about Bob and the man he had betrayed, his description of the man he had spied on the Nichols cottage on Thursday, a description tallying in every respect with the disguise Bob had worn when he was killed; Dave's identification of Lou Nichols as Bob's victim, "identification positive," he had said.

Lieutenant Carrigan sat back, relaxed and at ease, making no comment except for an occasional question to clarify a point. The young policeman who took notes seemed far more excited than he did. Perhaps, Janice thought, the lieutenant, like Timberlake, had outlived surprise.

Then, with a faint blush, she told him of her tentative identification of Sonia Strunski as the woman with whom Bob had had an appointment last Tuesday, the bronze hairpins, the jade ring, the fact that she had been in New York both on Tuesday and on Friday, on which occasion her jealous husband had been with her.

"Jealous husband?" Carrigan interrupted. "How jealous?"

"How can I tell? One of my neighbors said he was going to take a knife to her someday, or something like that. She said he's too vain to be willing to be made a fool of in public."

"Most men are," the lieutenant informed her dryly.

When she had finished her account, she made a little gesture and dropped her hands in her lap. The lieutenant noticed that she had discarded her wedding ring.

"I don't know," she said, "whether any of this is useful or whether it is just more red herrings. But I'd hate to have poor Lou involved if he should be in the clear, after what he has already suffered."

"One thing is clear, Miss Edwards. Your husband's murderer must have stood in line to wait his turn. It would be hard to think of anyone who managed to make so many bitter enemies in the span of thirty years. But there are a couple of suspects you are soft-pedaling, aren't there?"

The long hazel eyes, fringed with dark lashes, regarded him in surprise. What lovely eyes the girl had, but she seemed unaware of their effect; certainly she did not exploit them as most women would have done.

"This Mr. McClintock who identified Maxwell as the traitor, and who refused to shake hands with him, who would have accused him publicly if he hadn't felt so indebted to you—how deeply did he resent your husband?"

"Well, of course, when he first told us about the treachery and poor Lou being tortured, he was terribly upset. He'd just come out of prison camp himself, you know, and he is easily excited. That's why Fitz was so anxious to find him a quiet place where he could live and work without being subjected to the pressures of city life. He was worried about him."

"Does McClintock strike you as a violent person?"

"I suppose anyone can be violent, given reason enough," and Janice thought of Thomas threatening to kill Lou if she married him.

"And Mr. Fitzgerald?"

"Oh, that's really preposterous. It's not even worth discussing."

"But it's bound to be discussed, sooner or later, you know, and that alibi of his for Friday afternoon isn't worth a damn."

"But I know Fitz."

The handwriting expert opened the door, "Maxwell signed the traveler's checks, no question." He withdrew.

As though there had been no interruption the lieutenant said, "You thought you knew Maxwell." When Janice was silenced he drove his point home. "How much do you know about Lou Nichols? How much about Dave McClintock? How much about Hal Streichen? Would you have taken him for the kind of man who would introduce someone to you for money? How much about the Strunskis, either or both?" He went on remorselessly, "How much do you know about Bessie Maxwell or Pia Jensen, both of whom you seemed willing to take under your wing?"

"All right," she conceded, "I'm a fool about people."

He relented. "As long as you remember that." Then he smiled and held out his hand. "Don't worry about the inquest. It will be cut and dried. They will probably ask you about that telephone call your husband received at the Gotham. Then they'll adjourn. But don't make any bright suggestions or volunteer anything. Huh? Keep it simple. We have a long way to go yet, unless we get a break, though that happens more often than you might think. Just don't confuse the issue."

II

The receptionist at the apartment building welcomed with relief Miss Edwards's telephone call to inquire about her mail.

"We have a whole armful of letters and messages. We'll send them up at once."

The boy who rang the bell really did have an armful of mail. He gave her a quick, curious look and turned away. Janice dumped the load on the desk in the living room and then sorted it: letters in one place, bills in another, telephone messages in a third.

She wrote answers to the letters of condolence, grateful for a task that kept her busy and occupied her mind. The bills she dispatched in a hurry, thinking that it was pleasant to know she could pay everything without difficulty, that behind her there was a firm backlog that would last for the rest of her life, which reminded her that she had not talked to her lawyers about the affair.

She called and arranged for a meeting on Friday morning, when she would sign her will and take up in detail her plans for a foundation or trust fund to finance the colony at Inspiration Lake and arrange for a competent architect to design other cottages. The search for suitable applicants would have to await another year, when provisions for them had been made.

The senior partner told her that he was appalled to learn of her husband's murder. "You should have informed us of your impending marriage," he said reproachfully. After a few questions he assured her that he and the junior partner would attend the inquest with her. "As friends, of course," he said.

Only when she had put down the telephone did Janice wonder what he had meant. Did Perkins feel that it would be unwise for the widow of a murdered man to appear at an inquest with a battery of lawyers? Oh, nonsense; no one could conceivably believe that she had killed her bridegroom.

As she stamped the last letter, she heaved a sigh of relief and looked proudly at her cleared desk. There was nothing left except the briefcase in which she carried scripts back and forth when office work kept her too busy during the day for her reading. She must have been in a daze, she thought with wry amusement, to bring home scripts to read on her wedding night.

She opened the case and pulled out three scripts. There were two Gothics, *The Widow of Hindleston* and *Briarcliff Manor,* and beneath them a third script which she had not seen before, a battered script, which, her now experienced eyes told her, had made the rounds of established publishers before coming to Fitzgerald. The title was *A New Song for Ophelia* and clipped to it was a scrawled note:

> They sent this as a last resort, but I think it has a lot of promise. Offbeat but genuine emotion and an appealing situation. Enough guts to escape being pixie. You wanted to graduate from Gothics. This is your chance. Fitz."

The telephone rang and Lieutenant Carrigan informed her that the inquest had been postponed until Wednesday at three, which meant that the funeral service would have to be set ahead for Thursday. As it was to be completely private, this presented no difficulty.

When she came back from the telephone, she settled down with the script. She broke off only to order a light supper from the restaurant on the ground floor of the building and then returned to the script. It had an odd, haunting quality that held her. Offbeat, of course, and salesmen are unhappy when there isn't a neat label for their wares; and all new novels, unless sensational or sex-ridden, are difficult to sell. In any case Fitz really couldn't afford to take such a gamble.

Suppose, she thought, she were to offer to go into partnership with Fitz? With her money he would be able to expand and to take chances on books he'd be proud of or authors to whom he would like to give a break. He could ride the storm even if more bookstores went to the wall. It would be a useful venture and creative. And it would, she thought irrelevantly, be heaven to have a secure future, working and laughing and fighting with Fitz. Of course, he might not relish having her in a position of authority, but she would never put her judgment ahead of his.

She was still thinking of the idea when she went to bed and it was her first thought when she got up in the morning. After breakfast she finished the script and wrote a careful but enthusiastic report. Then, impulsively, she packed the briefcase and left the apartment, after instructing the maid supplied by the management—she ought to call the maid she had dismissed and apologize for her suspicions—to call Goodwill Industries and turn over to them all the men's clothing in the guest bedroom.

When she entered the office, she saw Fitz standing at the window in his room looking out into the dingy court. His hands were thrust into his pockets, his shoulders were stooped. He turned as the door opened and she saw his face light up.

"Janice!" He came almost at a run to lift the hinged counter for her. "I didn't dream you'd come."

"I found these scripts on my desk." For the first time in their acquaintance she felt shy, almost self-conscious with him. "I thought I'd better bring them in." She added with a trace of her lovely smile, "Especially when you were generous enough to let me read some straight fiction."

His eyes searched her face and he was relieved at what he saw. He took the briefcase from her and pulled up a chair beside his desk. "Do you want to talk or would you rather not?" he asked with the straightforwardness that had been characteristic of their relationship from the first, which was what had anchored it so firmly.

"There really isn't much of anything to say, is there? Except, of course, that I made an awful fool of myself."

"No, you didn't. You don't even know yourself yet, girl. Did Dave tell you?"

"About Bob? Poor Dave. What a job to give him. But, in a way, it was just one more thing. Everything about Bob was a lie. I'm not grief-stricken, though I suppose people will expect me to be. More than anything, I am humiliated."

"You needn't be. Just because you are trusting—"

She stopped him with a little gesture. "Any woman would be humiliated. I was so stupid I shouldn't have been allowed out alone."

"Well, thank God it hasn't hurt you too much. I was afraid of that. Anyhow, it's over."

"Oh, it hurts," she assured him. "I don't think I know yet how much it hurts or will continue to hurt. For it isn't over. Someone murdered Bob. Someone shoved him out of a window after cracking his skull with a hammer." Her voice was almost matter-of-fact. She had herself under control now. "Until the police can find out who did that, it will never be over. And even then—even then it won't be over because there will be the inevitable punishment to follow."

Fitz leaned forward, his long fingers closing over her hand. Then he jerked away as though he had been burned, and pushed his chair farther back, almost using his desk as a barricade between them.

"Are the police still interested in me as a possible suspect?" he asked conversationally.

"In you," she agreed in the same tone, "as well as," she counted on her fingers, "Bob's sister-in-law, who is glad he is dead and with justification; his typist and former mistress, who was not prepared for his marriage; Lou Nichols, whom Dave has identified as the prisoner of war whom Bob betrayed, and now at his mother's cottage at

Inspiration Lake; Sonia Strunski, who visited my apartment with Bob last Tuesday—good heavens, that's just a week ago today!—and to whom he gave a valuable jade ring; her husband, who has become weary of his wife's infidelities and who was in New York on Friday. There are also some unidentified men working a smuggling game with Bob; and, of course, there may be others: an uninhibited female who wrote him a letter like burning lava, and a former army colleague who more or less threatened blackmail."

"That's quite a record. How not to make friends. But what I want to know is, how deeply involved is Dave?"

"I don't know."

"And this man Lou? Could he have done it?"

"I don't see how anyone could have killed Bob," Janice said. "He was in disguise, which means he was prepared for trouble, and I can't understand how he could have been taken by surprise, off guard."

"But someone did take him off guard."

"I know. But if it was Lou, his mother and brother would be bound to know of his long absence from home and they would protect him; they'd lie themselves deaf and blind for him. Actually, his brother Thomas urged me to stay away from the lake for a while. So did Dave."

"Then they must believe you are in danger. For God's sake, Janice, be careful." Fitz left his barricade and came to her chair. She was on her feet, waiting for him, and stepped into his arms as naturally as though she had done it a hundred times before.

"I'm so horribly in love with you," he groaned as he released her.

"Fitz, this is an awful thing. Less than a week ago I was married, two days later my husband was murdered. And now—"

"This is the only thing that is right about the whole business. But, of course, it can't go on. I can see that now. Not now. Not yet. Not until the whole filthy situation is cleared up and there is no shadow of suspicion left to make a barrier between us." He pushed her back into her chair, returned to his own.

For a moment they looked at each other in wonder and in delight.

"I wish to God I'd asked you to marry me two months ago. But I thought you were just finding yourself and I ought to wait."

"You wanted to marry me then?"

"You're in my blood and I'll never get you out. But I messed things up, didn't I?" He broke off. "How arrogant I sound. As though all I had to do was ask and you would fall into my arms."

"I believe I would have," she told him, "only I never knew it before. I think I've loved you from the beginning, but we laughed so much, it all seemed so natural, so without tensions or problems—"

"Can't love be like that? Simple, natural, uncomplicated?"

"Of course it can. No, Fitz, don't kiss me again now. Please."

"Wait for the air to clear? But suppose it doesn't?"

"It must." She looked at her watch. "I've hardly time for lunch."

"Come with me."

She shook her head. "Not now. Not yet. I've got to go to the inquest. Wish me luck, Fitz."

TWELVE

BOTH LAWYERS were waiting for her and sat beside her in the unimpressive little room where the inquest was to be held. She was aware of the stir of interest occasioned by her appearance and by the cameramen and reporters held at bay by a policeman.

Later, most of the proceedings were a blur in her memory. There was testimony as to the discovery of the body of Robert Maxwell, fallen from the twelfth floor of the Grand Hotel to his death on the sidewalk. A doctor testified to his findings and a policeman reported that the man had been in disguise at the time of his death and that he had been robbed.

"Mrs. Robert Maxwell."

Janice, tall and slim in her black dress, took the stand. Yes, she had identified the body as that of her husband, Robert Maxwell. She was asked to describe the events immediately following their marriage and related that her husband had claimed that he had to attend a meeting of business associates in Atlantic City and he had left her immediately after the ceremony.

A wave of laughter was checked by a gavel and Janice felt color burning in her cheeks.

"Go on, Mrs. Maxwell. And I warn the spectators that

there is to be no further outbreak or I will have the court cleared."

On Friday morning her husband had telephoned to say he was leaving Atlantic City by bus and that he would be with her in time for lunch.

"You were to lunch where?"

"At the Gotham at one."

"Who knew that Mr. Maxwell could be reached at the Gotham at that time?"

She should have expected that question. It was the core of the whole mystery. That had been the weak spot all along.

"My employer, Gamaliel Fitzgerald, and an author of his, Mr. David McClintock. They saw us there."

"And no one else?"

A dim memory stirred in Janice's mind. "Wait!" the voice that had been barely audible rang clear. "Wait! I had forgotten. Bob called me at the office to say he was coming and I suggested we lunch at the Gotham at one because it was a kind of established habit. But," she made a gesture with her hand as though grasping for something, "while I was talking with Bob, the office door opened and then, when I hung up and turned around to see who it was, the door had closed; no one was there. But someone had been there, someone who could easily have heard what I said over the telephone."

A few questions failed to elicit anything concrete. The line of questioning changed smoothly. "Do you know of anyone named M. Canning?"

That, Janice remembered, was the name under which Bob's murderer had registered at the hotel. She shook her head and, on demand, said aloud, "No, I never knew anyone of that name."

There was sibilant whispering when she was dismissed to return to her seat between the two lawyers. Slowly the facts that Bob had never gone to Atlantic City, that he had faked an alibi, that he was in disguise when he died, were all brought out, but nothing new emerged. The identity of M. Canning had not been established.

The surprising thing was the amount of evidence that was not discussed. There was nothing said about Bob's peculiar business associates, nothing about his infamous war record and Lou Nichols, nothing about Pia Jensen or Bessie Maxwell. The police were holding their hands.

The expected verdict came in: Murder by person or persons unknown. The inquest was adjourned *sine die*. As they took her out to the senior partner's car, the latter remarked gravely, "It is a great pity, Mrs. Maxwell, that you mentioned the incident of the opening door."

"That sounds like something out of a Conan Doyle story," she remarked.

"That is precisely the way it sounded."

As she gave him a startled glance, he said, "It impressed the jury, I am afraid, as a rather awkward and inept and wholly unconvincing attempt to cover for one of the very few people who knew of that lunch engagement."

"Anyone would think you suspected me of protecting my husband's murderer or even that I might have had a hand in his death."

"It is a great pity," Perkins told her heavily, "that you have no alibi for Friday afternoon. Perhaps, Mrs. Maxwell, you would be wise to consult a criminal lawyer. Such matters are outside the scope of this firm."

II

Janice had arranged for a simple service at the funeral parlor. When she arrived the next morning at ten, she discovered in dismay that her hopes for privacy were ill-founded. A mob had gathered outside the building, made up chiefly of women, some with small children clinging to their hands, and a few men, either of retirement age or the drifters one finds in every city.

Several policemen were keeping an eye on the crowd, which surged forward when Janice stepped out of the taxi. Cameras clicked, newsmen and the familiar voice of a woman television reporter, called to her:

"Mrs. Maxwell, have you any theory about your husband's death? . . . Why was he wearing a disguise? . . . Do you know why he wanted an alibi?"

To her relief Lieutenant Carrigan emerged from the crowd, gestured to a policeman to restrain the press, and led her inside. She was shaking with nerves and he escorted her solicitously to a chair in the dim room where an organ throbbed. There were only two other mourners, whom she recognized in surprise to be Bessie Maxwell and Pia Jensen. The former gave Janice a half-challenging, half-defiant look and then stared straight ahead of her. Pia Jensen, wearing an ill-fitting and shabby black dress, was wiping red and swollen eyes, looking at the closed coffin. She paid no attention to Janice at all. On the coffin there was a small bunch of roses, with a card reading, "Love from Pia."

I never thought of flowers, Janice admitted guiltily to herself.

The service was mercifully brief, the words from the Bible were beautiful and sober, and then the manager of the undertaking establishment closed his Bible, the organ began once more to play, and the lieutenant rose, standing beside Janice rather like a guard. Then she became aware that he was watching the approach of the two women.

"I meant to tell you," he said in a low tone, "we've found the company that rented a car to Mr. Maxwell. He picked it up on Wednesday afternoon and returned it on Friday about twelve-thirty. According to the mileage, he could easily have made the round trip to the Adirondacks. We're checking motels now to find out where he spent the night on Wednesday and Thursday."

The two women were near her now. Pia came first. She paused as though to speak and then simply smiled at Janice and went on, blowing her nose.

But Bessie stopped, looking from the lieutenant to Janice. As Carrigan made no attempt to move away, she said, "I'd like to talk to you, Janice." She added. "In private."

After a glance to ascertain her wishes, Carrigan shrugged and went out.

Once more Janice had to face a barrage of questions as she emerged from the dim room into the blazing light and heat and noise of the street. And then two policemen escorted her hastily across the sidewalk to a waiting taxi. She got in, followed by the tenacious Bessie.

"Will you come up to the apartment?" Janice asked. "It's cooler there."

"Okay." Bessie lapsed into silence and did not speak again until Janice had unlocked the door of her apartment and switched on the air conditioning. Bessie walked around slowly and then stood at the windows looking out on the magnificent view.

"It takes money to keep up a place like this. You're one of the lucky ones."

"I know I am," Janice admitted humbly, "though just now—"

"You trying to make me believe you're sorry Bob's dead? If you ask me, the only one who really cared was that blonde who was sort of sniffling to herself. One of his women, I suppose. Well, I can't afford to take off too much time. They aren't charging me for this time because it's the funeral of a relative. But I'm in trouble over this business, you know."

Today the dark roots of her hair showed more clearly than before. There was a kind of grimy look about her that was not so much a matter of actual uncleanliness as a general atmosphere of poverty and neglect.

"Well," and she took a long breath, "the police are just driving me crazy, questioning my boss at the laundromat, questioning the landlady where I live. They even have the nerve to be asking around about my friends and what I do and how I live and all like that. It's just plain degrading and besides," and her voice began to rise. "I could lose my job if this goes on, and then where will I be? It's not my fault. I had nothing to do with Bob's death. I was just unlucky enough to be his sister-in-law. And first thing you know I'll be penniless, and then what? What do you intend to do about it?"

There was a silence that remained unbroken while Janice could not keep still, the bold eyes.

"Let's have one thing clear," Janice said quietly. "I don't know just what you have in mind, but I will not pay blackmail. Make no mistake about that."

"There's no question of blackmail," Bessie said sullenly. "Only you've got the works. It wouldn't hurt you." There was a whine in her voice. "And it was your husband who got me into the fix I'm in now. You owe me something."

"I don't owe you a thing, Bessie. What Bob did to you was long before I ever knew him."

"Has anyone," and Bessie leaned forward, "been at you like they've been at me? You know what I mean. 'Where were you Friday afternoon?' I read about the inquest before I went to the funeral parlor this morning. It looks like you were doing your best to suggest that someone else was there. But there's just the three of you. So which one are you protecting?"

Janice's voice was still cool, her manner relaxed. "I didn't kill Bob. I waited for him all afternoon, all evening, waited—and waited." She remembered those long hours of growing tension, growing fear, and something of that memory was in her face for Bessie to read.

"Okay, so maybe you are in the clear at that. And you can go on living here like a queen and I go back to that hellish laundromat—if I don't lose my job because of all those policemen nosing around."

"I won't pay a cent of blackmail. Understand that, Bessie. But if there's any way I can help you get a better job, I'll try. What would you like to do?"

Bessie surprised her by answering promptly, "I'd like to be a waitress."

"For heaven's sake! Why? It's such hard work."

"I've thought about it a lot. In this job I got you meet mostly women. But in a restaurant you meet the lonely guys, the ones who want to talk a bit. Not a bar girl. Men don't marry them. Not a store clerk where I'd just see more women. But lonely guys in restaurants, you know, they may not want to get married but they're, you know, sort of sick and tired of not being married, if you know what I mean."

"And that's what you want? To be married?"

Bessie nodded emphatically.

"Even after your experience with Bob's brother?"

"Bruce would have been all right if Bob hadn't seen a chance to get him this rich wife."

"Why didn't Bob marry her himself?"

"He'd finished basic training and he was just waiting to be shipped overseas. But next time I'll be more careful."

"Perhaps," Janice suggested, though she did not relish the idea of having her sister-in-law in such close proximity, "I could talk to the management here. There's a restaurant downstairs, you know."

"Uh-uh." Bessie was emphatic in her rejection of the idea. "Not in a place like this. Too much money. Guys like that don't look for a wife among the waitresses. A smaller place, well, not necessarily smaller, you know, but not so expensive, if you know what I mean."

Janice thought of the inn at Inspiration Lake. The restaurant manager might know of a likely spot for a hardworking and not unattractive girl. In any case he would do his best to please the woman who now owned the inn.

"I have an idea and something might come of it." Janice glanced at her watch. "Would you care to lunch with me?"

"Well, thanks, but I can't. I've only got off until one." Bessie stood up. "Sorry I got off on the wrong foot, Janice, but you know how it is."

"I'll do what I can."

Bessie nodded. "Yeah, I think you mean it. So thanks a lot and good luck." She turned back at the door. "Good luck," she repeated. "I guess we both could use some."

The rest of the day was a repetition of the day following Bob's murder. Once more the apartment building was besieged by reporters and cameramen. Once more Janice barricaded herself and refused to take telephone calls.

At last, because the need to speak to him was more than she could resist, she called Fitz. By the cautious way he answered, she was aware that there was someone with him.

"Fitz, I realize you can't talk."

"Not very well."

"Send me something to read, to keep me busy. I'm going mad up here with the press besieging the building. Even," she managed a laugh, "some Gothics would be welcome."

"With great pleasure," he said promptly. "I'll get a messenger up to you right away."

The messenger arrived within an hour, carrying a large package. When Janice opened it, she found three manuscripts: a suspense novel, a biography, and a book on contemporary politics as affected by the Watergate scandals. Evidently her report had increased his respect for her judgment.

Attached to the scripts was a letter. What Fitz had not been able to say on the telephone he said now, in such words that Janice read them almost with disbelief. She threw out her arms in a wide exultant gesture.

"You don't know yourself, girl," Fitz had said.

Well, did she? She had been honest about her vulnerability where Bob was concerned. But what about Fitz? She had turned to him with the same faith, the same trust, the same illusion that she loved and was loved. In her case, indeed,

>   . . . the funeral bak'd meats
> Did coldly furnish forth the marriage tables.

What, after all, did she know about Fitz? He claimed that he had loved her for months, but it was only after she had informed him of the money she had left him in her will, only when by arranging to house Dave she had indicated the extent of her wealth, that he had showed any personal interest in her. That was the day he had first asked her to have a drink with him after work. If it hadn't been that she was to meet Bob, she would have done so. What then?

Lieutenant Carrigan had hammered home to her the point that she knew nothing about her fellow man. She picked up the cigarette lighter from the desk and touched the flame to the edge of Fitz's letter, dropped it into a big ashtray, and with a letter opener crushed out the burned fragments. And then, of course, she regretted her action and wanted the letter back.

That night the television news showed the crowd outside the funeral parlor, showed her, looking to her own jaundiced eyes ten feet tall, being led out of the place by two policemen, for all the world, she thought, as though I were under arrest.

Next morning, she discovered in relief that the patient watchers had withdrawn, so she was unaccompanied when she went to keep her appointment with her lawyers. She was unsure of her status, uncertain of her welcome. So far she had pushed aside the implications of the senior partner's comment to her about hiring a criminal lawyer, as though she might be involved in some way with Bob's murder. The idea was too fantastic to be taken seriously.

When she was seated in Perkins's office, with Scott a grave but silent witness, she put the question bluntly.

"I realized Wednesday after I left you that you believed I would need a criminal lawyer. I would like to know, please, whether you suspect me of having any part in my husband's death or any knowledge of it, either before or after the fact?"

This approach was unexpected and unwelcome. The two men consulted one another with a glance. Then the senior bent over his desk, looking steadily at Janice. At length he nodded his head.

"I believe you are in the clear. Naturally, there were some circumstances, some puzzling details. The police have been here asking questions."

"Tell them whatever they want to know, of course. I have nothing to hide. If you doubt that, please say so and I'll look elsewhere for a lawyer. If you have any question in your mind about my innocence, if you cannot trust my word, it would be better for all of us if I seek another lawyer."

Perkins put up a restraining hand. "Let's consider the situation carefully. It is too important for a rash or hasty decision. But there are, of course, some factors. For instance that bequest to Mr. Fitzgerald. The police naturally wanted to see your will and it aroused some speculation."

"Yes, I know," Janice admitted. "I am almost tempted to ask you to cut it out of the will but, if I do that, the police will be bound to think that he may be involved in this business. So let it stand for a time. Is there anything else that made you—uncertain about me?"

"That unlikely comment about the opening door."

"But it was true, Mr. Perkins. It happened. Whoever opened the door went away. But it was open during my conversation with Bob."

"Of course you are aware that there isn't an iota of proof that anyone ever did open the door. Certainly there is not a scrap of evidence that whoever opened the door went to the Grand Hotel, took a room in the name of M. Canning, telephoned Maxwell at the Gotham, put up a convincing story to get him there, and then smashed him over the head and sent him hurtling out of a window, after having robbed him."

"No proof at all," Janice agreed. "But M. Canning did call him, did kill him, and rob him, and push him out of a window. What I can't possibly understand is how anyone was able to hit Bob on the head with a hammer. He was in disguise; he was prepared for trouble. Can you see a man in his position turning his back to someone with a hammer?"

"That has the police guessing too," the senior partner admitted. "Well, I expect we had better leave it to them. They seem to be efficient men who know their job. Now about this art colony of yours—" He pulled out a pad of paper. "It's going to be an expensive deal, you know. Only you can decide just how expensive and extensive it is going to be."

"How much do you think I am worth at this moment?"

After a little hesitation Perkins suggested a tentative figure. "More or less, of course. More or less."

"Good heavens! Well, to start with myself, I'd like a pleasant life and to know I can pay my bills. But I don't want that kind of money. I don't need star sapphires and oceangoing yachts, or my own jet to take me to England to catch the opening of a new play. Just a pleasant income. I wouldn't be a star attraction then, which, considering what an idiot I've made of myself, is just as well."

The senior partner made soothing noises.

"Let's say twenty cottages in all," Janice decided. "We can put a time limit on people staying there to give more artists a chance and not make it possible for anyone to encroach, unless— Perhaps I should retain the final decision on that." She thought of Jake Peters.

"That can be done well within the limit we had set," Perkins said in relief. "What else?"

Janice thought of the partnership she would like to establish with Fitz. Thought of it with such longing that it was like pain. But not now. Not yet. Never, perhaps.

"Just so my will can be in order in case of disaster," she said, "I will leave the residue of the estate temporarily for medical research, not buildings and fanfare, but to support the real work. No one, at least, would want to kill me for that, would they?"

The senior partner found nothing to say.

THIRTEEN

WHEN SHE RETURNED to the penthouse, the telephone was ringing.

"Janice," Fitz said, his voice strained, "I've just had a call from Dave. He seems to be in a tailspin. The local police up there are questioning him about Maxwell and checking on his movements last Friday. If it had come at any other time, he might have taken it in his stride, but because of his prison experiences, he is still as jittery as hell."

"Fitz, do you think it is possible he has a reason for being afraid?"

"I don't know. The thing is that he more or less relies on me, and this call was a kind of S O S. God knows I have wanted to keep out of the picture entirely on your account, but I can't see any other way. I've got to go up there. Of course I'll do my damnedest to keep out of sight, and Dave says he can put me up. I just thought I ought to tell you."

"Then I think I'd better go, too."

"You keep away," Fitz said sharply. "You've been warned not only by Dave but by that other fellow up there."

"Thomas? Well, yes, but nothing is going to happen to me and there's something I want to do."

"Don't be a fool, girl."

"Fitz, if Dave is really under suspicion, there is something I'll have to find out. I want to see for myself what shape Lou is in. Did Dave tell you where to get the plane? Then I'll see you there." She broke the connection before he could protest and ran to get her coat and check her handbag. On her last trip she had left enough clothes and cosmetics so that she no longer needed to carry a suitcase.

There was an unusually large crowd waiting at the plane and Janice recalled Vladimir Strunski's party. At least there was safety in numbers. With so many people milling around, she would not be noticed when she went to the Nichols cottage and it was unlikely that Fitz's presence would be observed at all, or he would be taken for one of Strunski's guests, few of whom knew each other.

Whether because of Strunski's reputation or Sonia's charms, the group was a distinguished one. Aside from Golschmann, with his big head and the powerful shoulders which seemed to propel him along, as she had seen him cross a concert stage many times, there was a famous woman actress, a male musical comedy star, several musicians identified by the violin cases they clung to, several well-known figures from outside the arts: a diplomat who had recently published a distinguished book of memoirs, written with taste and wit, and a crusading senator.

Hal Streichen, as usual, had sauntered up to the waiting crowd. When he saw Janice, he swerved cautiously away and attached himself to Thomas, a drawn and haggard Thomas. Janice was relieved that he had not seen her. He would not be pleased that she had disregarded his advice. But if his alarm was on Lou's account, it was high time to know the truth. Dave must not be sacrificed to protect Lou.

Fitz detached himself from the crowd and started toward her, remembered, and turned back. Only his eyes met hers for one long satisfying moment. She was mistaken about Thomas being unaware of her presence. He had seen her approach, seen the tall man's impulsive movement toward her, the way he had checked himself, and the look they had exchanged. They might as well have kissed, he thought, and he stumbled blindly getting on the plane, arousing the inevitable comment from Hal about his drinking habits.

For once in his sober life Thomas wished that he could get drunk, run away from the intolerable, escape from this unbearable pain. He wished he need no longer hold down with an iron hand this seething volcano within him, but let the damned thing explode, go up like Vesuvius. The very thought of it was exhilarating. But from force of habit his face was expressionless, his voice muted, as he parried Hal's remarks and settled down with the evening paper.

Several of the passengers recognized Janice from newspaper pictures and her involuntary appearance on television, but they were too well-bred to stare and she was left mercifully alone until Golschmann came purposefully down the aisle to ask her neighbor politely to change seats, and turned his big, ugly face to Janice. He had a wide smile and displayed somewhat badly treated teeth. He put his square muscular artist's hands on hers.

"Well, my dear, Vladimir assured me that you were going to be at the lake, so I planned something special for you. I'm doing a Beethoven sonata for the good of my soul, and some Liszt for people who hate music, but in between and just for you the *Gaspard de la Nuit*, so if you don't come to hear me, I shall feel neglected."

"I'm sorry," she told him, "it won't be possible."

"Nothing is impossible. What am I to do if you aren't there? Who else is going to like the Ravel? I haven't played it in years and I polished it just for you."

Janice surrendered. "You are incredibly kind."

"Nonsense. Remember that year I had rheumatism in my hands and couldn't even practice, let alone concertize. Your stepfather made me a loan that carried me nicely until I was back on my feet—or should I say my hands?—again?"

"I'll bet," Janice said dryly, "he charged fifteen per cent interest."

"That is neither here nor there. The point is that a pianist with crippled hands is a damned poor bank risk. So you'll come listen tomorrow night? If I can't lure you by myself, we're going to do the 'Archduke' and a gay little Haydn trio."

Dave was waiting at the plane. He waved as he caught sight of Fitz, who gave an exclamation of irritation as he went to greet him, raising his brows in a gesture of resignation as he passed Janice. But Dave's capacity for blunder was infinite.

"Hi, Janice! Let me drive you home. I don't see your station wagon and Helen Peters lent me her car. Get in. Get in. You and Fitz are both so thin we can all sit in front."

"There are times," Fitz said, his voice low but with so savage an expression that Dave was startled, "when your lack of elementary common sense is terrifying."

"But what—" Dave was bewildered.

"The last thing I wanted was to be known to be with you or to have Janice associated with either of us up here in any way. Well, you've wrecked that." Seeing Dave's look of chagrin, he relented. "All right. Water over the dam. Let's let the whole thing drop. Janice, you didn't tell me how lovely this place is and how immense."

Dave drove up to Peaceful Haven with a flourish. Fitz, after getting an impression of the big rambling house, gave her an odd look. "You're full of surprises, aren't you?"

Lights flashed on and Bertie came hurrying out. "Miss Edwards! We didn't expect you."

"I didn't have time to call you, but it doesn't matter. Mr. McClintock gave me a lift. And if Mrs. Bertie worries about food, all I want is a salad or an omelet and some iced coffee. I'm too tired to cope with more." She waved to Dave and Fitz and went inside.

II

That evening the sky clouded over and there were distant rumbles of thunder. The air was as heavy, as hard to breathe, as it had been in New York, so oppressive that a weight seemed to press on Janice's chest, a band tightened around her head. She went to bed early, taking a couple of aspirin tablets, and she lay tossing from side to side, while the storm increased, until she had a raging headache.

The storm gathered force, the roll of thunder was incessant, lightning flashed, and then there was a terrific clash of thunder and lightning came jagging out of the sky. There was a crash. Janice thought the house had been struck, but next morning she discovered that a fir tree, one that was usually decorated for Christmas, had been split by the lightning and half the trunk riped away.

And the rain came in a torrent, pounding on the roof, rushing through the gutters, and gradually the air grew less oppressive. At length Janice slept, a heavy, unrestful sleep.

The headache still remained in the morning, not acute as it had been the night before, but a constant throbbing so that with every step she took she felt a jolt of pain. All the fatigue of the past week seemed to drop on her at once. She managed to drink a cup of black coffee and eat a piece of cantaloupe, but she pushed aside the rest of the breakfast Mrs. Bertie had provided.

"You don't look well, and that's a fact. And small wonder after what you've been through. Don't you want me to call Dr. Willis? He still makes house calls in an emergency. Or Bertie could drive you over there. He has office hours from ten to twelve every morning."

Janice shook her head. "There's nothing wrong but a headache and fatigue."

"I suppose," Mrs. Bertie said, troubled, "you really ought to lie down. That's what they say, of course. But in my opinion you'd be better off if you get out of doors. It's a beautiful day after the storm, as though the world had just had its face washed."

"That's an idea." Janice went out onto the screened porch and sat looking at the lake that dazzled under the morning sun. The air was spicy with the scent of pine and spruce and balsam. She would have liked to sit here in a kind of lethargy, not doing anything; above all, not thinking about anything. Wherever her thoughts turned, they came upon a dead end.

But she had come here for a purpose. Either Dave or Lou must have killed Bob. There was no possible alternative. Unquestionably, Fitz was deeply worried about Dave, and his anxiety had brought him here to the lake to see for himself what the truth was and find out why Dave should be so upset by what appeared to be only routine police questioning.

But the more likely one was Lou, who had suffered so horribly because of Bob's treachery, and who might, besides, resent him because Janice had married him, though the latter was less likely, unless Lou had changed greatly. And that was what she had come to find out. The truth about Lou.

She passed the Strunski house, deserted because, no doubt, they were both at the inn attending to their guests and making final arrangements for the night's party.

She passed the Peters cottage, where there was no sign of life, and went on, walking toward the Nichols cottage. Thomas came out and she ducked out of sight behind a bush, her heart pounding wildly, which was ridiculous. Who could be afraid of Thomas? To her amazement he got into Lou's car and drove away. When he was gone, she stepped back on the path. The windows were open and she saw Grace in the kitchen, sliding a cake into the oven, intent on what she was doing. Janice peered into the living room and the bedroom windows. With the exception of Grace, the cottage was empty. For a moment she was puzzled. Then she recalled that Helen Peters had seen Lou out walking. She left the cottage and followed the path that went along the edge of the lake. From where she was she could see for nearly half a mile. There was no one in sight. She turned back and took the first path that led into the woods, a path beaten by poor Llewellyn Nichols when he was in search of ideas for the great American novel, which had never materialized.

Around a small clump of pines she came upon Lou, sitting on a tree stump, attentively watching a woodpecker earning its supper the hard way. As the bird hauled out a worm, Lou laughed with pleasure. It was a child's laugh.

"Hello, Lou," she said, and he turned around. Lou? Yes, of course. Lou, thinner, browner, but with an underlying pallor below the tan. Lou, smiling at her with a child's smile, looking at her with a child's eyes.

"Hello." After a minute he said, "Oh, it's Janice. That's good." He looked around craftily. "Janice, I want to whittle," and he held out a stick, "but they won't let me have a knife." He looked at her, aggrieved. To her horror, tears twinkled on his lashes.

I think, she told herself fiercely, if Bob did that to Lou, I could kill him myself.

She sat down on a flat stone and explained that she didn't have a knife—girls never did, he agreed in disappointment—and asked him what he had been doing. She was careful about how she phrased her words.

His face clouded. "They won't let me do anything I want. When I get out, they always come running. Every time. But I fooled them the other day." He laughed happily and a ripple of fear ran down Janice's spine, the reaction of the normal for the abnormal. He leaned forward, a lock of hair falling over his eyes, smiling. "We've always been good friends, haven't we?"

"Always," she assured him.

"Lou!" Grace called. "Lou!"

He put his finger to his lips, shook his head, laughing at Janice with a trace of his old mischief.

"Lou!" Grace was frantic.

Then she came running through the woods, her hair falling down, her apron torn on a branch. She put her hand on Lou's shoulder and he screamed. The sound was horrifying.

"Lou! It's Mother. It's Mother."

Gradually the scream died away and he got up, letting her lead him back to the cottage. Over her shoulder she said, "You see what you've done?"

For a long time Janice sat there until the heat of the sun on her unshaded head brought back the pain. So that was what had happened to Lou. One thing was clear. He could not have been the one who planned Bob's murder. He was incapable of planning anything. Abruptly she leaned against a tree and retched.

FOURTEEN

DAVE WAS ON the telephone when Janice got back to the house. "I'm sorry as hell. I seem to have messed everything up, meeting you like that. But it won't matter in the long run because we've got to meet tonight anyway. Sinuous Sonia has called three times to make sure that I bring my house guest to the clambake. I've heard through the grapevine that you'll be there, so I thought I'd issue a fair warning."

"Don't worry about it too much," Janice said. "Oh, Dave, I've seen Lou."

"You have!"

"And talked to him."

"I didn't have a chance. Did you learn anything?"

"I learned what I came here to find out," she said, her voice so sober that he was startled. "Lou didn't kill Bob. His mind has been practically destroyed. He's like a small boy, incapable of planning or carrying through that murder. Even if he recognized Bob when he came up here—and I doubt it; I imagine the war is blotted out and he has only childhood memories—it would have made no difference. Lou is innocent of that murder, Dave."

"You sound—you think I—" Dave sounded dazed.

"I don't know what to think."

By five the headache had dwindled to a slight nagging

discomfort that she could ignore, and she decided, after all, to go to the Strunski party, especially since Golschmann had prepared the Ravel for her. And then she recognized the pretext for what it was. She wanted to see Fitz. And if she sat in the background and simply listened to the music, there would be nothing for anyone to criticize.

"I'll get a lift home," she told Bertie when he left her at the inn. "You won't need to wait up for me. Good night."

The inn was ablaze with lights and crowded with men and women in evening dress, for the Strunski parties were formal now as they had been in Europe, a matter which pleased the manager of the inn, who was Swiss-trained, and who could not reconcile himself to the hippie attire which younger people occasionally introduced into the lobby and even attempted to wear in the dining room. On the balcony the orchestra was playing softly.

Near the door Sonia and Vladimir stood receiving their guests, as they had taken over the inn for the occasion. Sonia was splendid in a black evening dress with diamond eardrops, a diamond necklace, and the jade ring. Beside her Strunski, the only man in a white tie, as the others had settled for dinner jackets, looked rather like a penguin, though he had an unquestioned dignity that owed nothing to the row of medals across his chest.

Strunski saw Janice first and turned to welcome her. "Golschmann promised me that you would be here," he said, shaking hands warmly. "It was good of you to come."

"It was kind of you to let me come." Janice turned to Sonia, who did not notice her until her husband touched her arm, as she was engrossed in conversation with the musical comedy star who still played youthful roles and whose fine baritone voice had not deteriorated, but who, when seen at close range, resembled Dickens's description of Harold Skimpole, who "had more the appearance, in all respects, of a damaged young man than of a well-preserved elderly one." He was listening to his hostess with flattering attention.

Over her shoulder Sonia smiled and nodded at Janice,

blew her a kiss, and returned to her conversation, while Strunski watched, intent and unsmiling.

As she saw Thomas bearing down purposefully on her, Janice in relief joined Helen and Jake Peters, who were wearing the same evening clothes they had appeared in for the past ten years, rustier and, in Jake's case, tighter-fitting.

Jake nodded in approval. "I'm glad you came tonight. Very sensible of you."

"Rather foolhardy, isn't it?" Janice retorted. "People are bound to gossip."

"You can't live according to what people will think of you. Remember what Emerson said: 'It's a life I lead, not an apology.' Anyhow it is perfectly legitimate to listen to fine music."

"I must say," Helen told her candidly, "I've never seen you look so well."

"Or so well-dressed?" Janice said with a smile, aware that the long white dress was becoming.

"There's that, of course. I do love pretty clothes. Don't you?"

"But only from a distance," Jake said bitterly. "You've never had a chance to own any."

"I have everything I want," she told him fiercely. "Oh, dear, here comes Thomas with a look of determination on his face."

"Then it must be for the first time in his life," Jake commented.

Perhaps it was unfortunate that Thomas's approach coincided with the arrival of Dave and Fitz. Before Thomas could speak, Dave said, "Mrs. Peters, do let me introduce my friend and publisher, Gamaliel Fitzgerald. And Mr. Peters, Fitz. Someday I hope he will show you some of his work. I've seen a painting that Janice has bought. A lovely thing. Haunting."

Janice nodded casually to the two men, aware that her color was rising especially when she met Fitz's eyes. She knew that she had never looked better in her life and the knowledge made her look still better. There were no words exchanged between them, but Helen Peters looked from face to face, her eyes widening. Her attitude was one of alarm rather than one of pleasure and, as always when she felt uncertain, she took an involuntary step toward her husband as though for guidance and support.

It was Thomas, moving with uncharacteristic purposefulness, who broke up the little group. "Yours is a daiquiri, I think," he said to Janice, thrusting a frosty glass into her hand. "I want to talk to you." Without giving her a chance to answer, he led her to one of the small tables for two that had been set out under the balcony.

Fitz looked after them, his eyebrows arched. "Who is that?"

"That," Jake told him, "is the masculine equivalent of Patient Griselda. His name is Thomas Nichols and he appears to be laboring under the strange belief that the proper time to stake his claim to a woman is just two days after she has buried her husband. How very like Thomas that is."

But Thomas was not staking a claim. He took a long pull at a mild Scotch and water and said abruptly, "So now you know."

"I'm sorry," Janice said inadequately. "Terribly sorry. Can't anything be done?"

Thomas shrugged. "The doctors don't seem to think so. Lou wasn't the kind to stand up to torture, I suppose."

"No one is," Janice said indignantly.

"If only he hadn't tried to escape from prison camp! But Lou never could stand any discipline. So far as I can make out, he was always in hot water during the fighting. So when they tortured him, he broke completely."

The story that had seemed horrible when told by Dave was even worse in Thomas's unemotional voice. A strange new Thomas.

"Well, instead of dying, as anyone would expect, Lou was picked up by some natives who looked after him until it was safe to get in touch with our forces. His hands had been—badly mangled—so there was a fingerprint problem and it took some time to get an identification. All he could remember himself was that he was called Lou. He was put in a hospital for mental patients. When he's happy, he laughs a lot. But after a while he begins to cry for his mother. That's why the authorities suggested letting him go home, an experiment to see whether Mother's presence would be beneficial. It isn't, of course I knew that from the beginning. But you can't make Mother believe anything she doesn't want to believe.

"Of course, Lou will have to go back. He'll probably be institutionalized for the rest of his life. Naturally the government will pay for that. I'd like to persuade Mother to live somewhere near him so she can see him as often as she likes. But I can hardly suggest it now while she is still coming to terms with his condition. You see that, don't you, Janice?"

"Of course," she said readily. "Surely you didn't think I would ask you to move."

"These days I don't know what to expect of you. Why did you come up here this weekend? I thought you were going to stay away for a while."

She couldn't, Janice realized, tell Thomas she had come up to see for herself whether Lou had been capable of murdering her husband. "There are a number of problems to handle," she said, "until the estate is put in shape." The little glow occasioned by seeing Fitz had faded and the headache was nagging at her, pulsing behind her eyes, throbbing on top of her head, making her feel slightly nauseated.

"I was surprised," Thomas said in a tone of strong disapproval, "that you would consent to come to a party so soon—though that is your business."

"Yes, it is my business, but I won't stay long, not for the whole concert. I have a bad headache."

"Do you—take things for headaches?"

She recalled that his father had committed suicide by taking some kind of painkiller; the exact medicine had never been made public. He was watching her in a curiously intent manner.

"Just aspirin." She was relieved when a general stir

through the room indicated that the party was moving toward the dining room. She found Dave at her side.

"I'm taking you in." He grinned. "I think Sonia got ideas when you were so eager to come into the cottage with me."

"I understood that she had ideas of her own."

"Cat," he said. "I'm afraid I don't have what it takes," and he indicated the musical comedy star who was placed at Sonia's left. She had Golschmann at her right. Janice noticed that Fitz had been paired with Helen Peters. Evidently uncertain of his status, Sonia had placed him beside the woman whom she regarded as most negligible. They would enjoy each other, she thought.

Like all Strunski parties, this one was gay, with good talk interlarded with laughter but none of the set jokes—"Have you heard this one?"—which are so fatal to good talk. Strunski was a superb host, in spite of his somewhat kingly manner, and Sonia was at her best in a situation of this sort, the perfect hostess.

As soon as she had released Golschmann, he turned to Janice with a groan. "This is torment," he declared bitterly. "Because I am to play I cannot eat, I cannot drink. The wine is superlative; you can count on Vladimir for that. And I with a great body to feed can only nibble. It's enough to make me swear off playing."

She laughed at him. "I've known you too long. As soon as the music is over, you will begin to eat—and eat—and eat."

"But meantime." He picked up a glass of claret, sniffed at its aroma, and put it down with a groan. Then he said quietly, "My dear, because I act like a mountebank does not mean that I am unaware of what has been happening to you."

She checked him with a swift gesture. "Perhaps I should be horribly ashamed, but I am not grieving, Maestro. Horrified and shocked, yes. But not—not really unhappy."

"And for that I thank God," he told her. "But you must take care, you know. There are not many people who value honesty and fewer still who are comfortable when other people ignore the shibboleths."

When Sonia again claimed Golschmann, Janice turned to find Dave watching her expression. "Since we talked on the telephone I've been realizing that you are half inclined to think I killed Maxwell. I've thought and thought. I have no proof at all. But I'd be glad to take one of those truth serums or whatever they are so you could test for yourself whether I am lying. I don't know how to go about it, but I'll ask Fitz. He's bound to know."

Janice was unable to give him the answer he obviously wanted, to assure him that she believed in his innocence. Because if Dave were innocent, she was left with Fitz. And that was unbearable.

Once more the party broke up to reassemble in the ballroom in which the concert was to take place. In the general shifting of people Fitz went to take Dave's place beside Janice. She welcomed him with a smile but it faded when he said, "Dave is afraid you think he killed Maxwell."

II

Golschmann had finished the Liszt sonata in a blaze of pyrotechnics, and after bowing, made his way out of the ballroom to mop his head and smoke a cigarette while the violinist and cellist who were to play the trios with him took their places and tuned their instruments.

In a general quest for cigarettes people drifted outside, breathing in the fresh, crisp mountain air that was refreshing after the rather airless ballroom.

Janice wandered aimlessly away from the inn with Fitz strolling beside her, hands in his pockets, until he noticed that she was shivering and then he put her cape over her shoulders.

"With that white dress covered up, there is nothing to be seen of you but a ghostly white face. An unreal face. Like a dead face rising out of a mist."

"Don't!" she exclaimed, and then Fitz gave a smothered

exclamation and caught her wrist, holding it so tightly that next day she found a black and blue mark on it. He had brought her to an abrupt halt. At first she was bewildered and then she saw Sonia in the arms of the musical comedy star, her face, lighted by a window, clearly visible as he bent to kiss her.

As Janice started a noiseless retreat, Fitz's grip tightened. Then she saw Vladimir Strunski, unaware of them, unaware of anything but the woman locked in the man's arms. The light from the window reflected on the barrel of the small automatic he was holding.

Fitz moved then. Two long steps and he knocked the gun out of the old man's hand, sent it rattling to the ground, scooped it up.

"You fool!" he said, his voice low. "You utter fool. What did you hope to accomplish by that?"

Sonia and the actor had leaped apart and turned startled faces toward them, Sonia's mouth opening and closing without a sound, the actor looking as though he wished he could take to his heels.

Strunski turned to Fitz. "I wasn't really going to kill them, you know. I just thought it was time to give Sonia a lesson." He flexed his right wrist in some alarm. "I hope to God you haven't lamed it. I'm giving a concert this winter. If you've lamed it—"

Obviously the condition of his wrist mattered a great deal more to him than his wife's amorous activities, and Fitz began to laugh. "Your wrist isn't injured. Where did you get this thing?" and he looked at the gun he was still holding.

"I picked it up at Peaceful Haven. Anyone can get in there, you know. They have so many guns I was sure Janice wouldn't mind."

"Suppose," Fitz suggested, "I return it for you."

"Thank you very much." Strunski gave him a courtly bow. "Now I must not neglect my guests. Golschmann will be ready to play the Archduke." He trotted back to the inn without another glance at his wife and the actor.

As the last thing Janice wanted at that moment was to

confront Sonia, she said quickly, "Will you take me home, Fitz? Jake Peters will lend you his car."

He was back in a few minutes, dangling the car keys. "The car is parked at the end of the lot. Wait here and I'll get it."

Thomas was standing on the inn porch watching, and Janice said hastily, "I'll go with you."

"I must say," Fitz commented mildly as he turned the key in the switch, "this is hardly an ideal resort of convalescents, is it? Old Faithful going off every hour. That man Nichols watching you; Strunski waving a gun at his erring wife. A gun!" He chuckled. "Did you notice that he was much more worried about his wrist than about his wife's activities?"

"Well, he's used to them and he didn't really intend to hurt them, just frighten them."

Fitz was amused. "I like your casual attitude. But, my dear girl, when a man shoots, he is more likely than not to hit something."

"Thank heaven that he didn't."

"What's really worrying you, Janice? Not Strunski and his fireworks."

"Down in my heart I've been hoping that Lou killed Bob. In a way I could understand that. But I've seen him. Lou is innocent; his brain has been destroyed."

"The poor devil!"

"Yes, the poor devil. So now, Fitz there are only three people who knew how and where to find Bob last Friday. Dave—and you—and me."

FIFTEEN

HERE WE GO round the mulberry bush, Janice thought wearily. Picture of a woman who can't learn by her mistakes. She moved carefully so as not to jolt her throbbing head, and wondered whether it would be better to risk making it worse by getting out of bed and prowling around her bathroom in search of aspirin, or whether it might go away if she lay still.

By now the party at the inn would be over. Dave and Fitz would have driven Jake and Helen back to their cottage and then walked on to their own, or perhaps Peters had suggested that they take the car and return it in the morning. What were they talking about? Dave or Fitz? One of them had killed Bob, must have killed Bob. Dave had a strong motive and he was still emotionally unstable because of his war experiences. If he had been driven to murder by his discovery of Bob's identity, the police would make some allowances, wouldn't they? Because, if it was Fitz, the only possible motive would be Janice's money.

Pain stabbed through her head and she slid her legs out of bed. She'd have to take something. That was when she heard the crash, and she found herself sitting bolt upright, her heart leaping in her breast. What—it must have been a dining room window. She groped for her robe and then remembered Fitz laughing about the distraught heroines in Gothic novels who were constantly rushing out into the dark, especially when danger threatened. What did they expect? They were simply asking for it.

She switched on the light and then opened her door cautiously. Then a door opened at the back of the hall and Bertie appeared, wrapped in a robe made of wide red and white stripes, carrying a small businesslike revolver.

"You get back into your room," he told her. He went steadily down the stairs, switched on lights, and then went into the dining room. After an interval he called to the anxious girl upstairs. "There's no one here, Miss Edwards, but maybe you'd better come down."

There was no one on the first floor except Bertie, who was standing in the big dining room where a vase of flowers had been knocked off the table by the gust of wind when the window had blown open. But it hadn't blown open, Bertie said. Someone had forced it.

"But what was it all about?" Janice demanded in bewilderment. "Why would a burglar break into this house, making such an uproar, when all he had to do was open the front door and walk in? So far as I can see, nothing has been taken."

"No," Bertie said slowly, "nothing was taken, but something was added, Miss Edwards." Following his gesture, Janice saw, propped against the big crystal punchbowl on the sideboard, a strip of cardboard on which letters had been pasted:

IF YOU WANT TO LIVE,
GO AWAY AND STAY AWAY.

"Well," she said breathlessly, "what a very unfunny joke."

"You go back to bed, Miss Edwards, I'll sit up for the rest of the night. I can catch up on sleep in the morning." He added, "I don't like it. Someone tried to scare you. I think we ought to call the state police." As she was hesitant, he added, "It's not just an isolated situation, is it? After all, someone murdered your husband. This may not be someone's idea of a joke."

While Bertie telephoned, Janice measured coffee and made some sandwiches, hoping they would soften the annoyance of the police at being called so far for so trivial a situation. Then she ran upstairs to change to a wool skirt and sweater, as the night had grown chilly. When she returned, she suggested that Bertie go up to change, but he shook his head.

"I'm not leaving you alone," he said firmly, his hand resting on the butt of the revolver.

"Where on earth did you get that?"

"There were some cat burglars at the inn a few years back and Mr. Ransome suggested I take one of his guns, just in case."

The state police, in accordance with Bertie's request, arrived without the use of sirens. Bertie, still in his garish bathrobe, went to the door, the gun in his hand. Then he stepped back with a little sigh of relief, which revealed to Janice how frightened the gallant elderly man had been, and let them in.

"You the one who made the call?" one of them asked.

"Yes, sir." Bertie told them of hearing the crash as the dining room window was forced open and seeing that Miss Edwards was about to go downstairs to investigate, he had insisted on going first. By the time he got downstairs, there was no one in the house and nothing had been taken.

"You called us just because a window blew open?"

"No, sir. The window was forced. Reason I called was because someone left this and made all that racket to make sure it was found." Bertie indicated the cardboard warning.

There was a moment's silence while the two men examined it without touching it. Then one of them smote himself on the forehead. "Of course. I should have made the connection. Inspiration Lake. You are Mrs. Maxwell, the new owner, and your husband was murdered last week. I'd have made the connection sooner, but this man called you Miss Edwards." His eyes narrowed as he took in the buttercup yellow sweater and skirt. Not much indication of mourning here, he thought.

At Janice's request Bertie brought in the tray of coffee and sandwiches and the men helped themselves liberally.

The older of the two asked, "Have you any idea who sent you this warning?"

Dave? Thomas? "No," she said. "I thought at first it was just a joke."

"Do you have any enemies here?"

"I shouldn't think so. After all, I've spent so little time up here, though I've known all the people in a way for years."

"One newcomer." The younger trooper opened a notebook. "Name of David McClintock. We've been doing a routine check on him at the request of the New York police. Seems he was in New York at the time of Mr. Maxwell's death last week."

"So," Janice informed him, "was practically everyone in the colony, so far as I can make out. But as none of them knew my husband—" Her voice trailed out. There was Hal Streichen, there was Dave, there was Sonia. And tonight Strunski had shown that he was capable of violence and that he was prepared to shoot the man who was having an affair with his wife.

I am trying to protect Bob's murderer, Janice admitted and that is inexcusable. There is no excuse for murder. But to involve the Strunskis, and perhaps cast a shadow on his great reputation in his last years; to involve Dave and, if he was innocent, leave a suspicion of guilt over him all his life—she couldn't do it.

When it became apparent that she had nothing more to contribute, the older man, after Bertie had refilled his coffee cup and passed more sandwiches, said, "Mrs. Maxwell—oh, I see you prefer to be called Miss Edwards—" He waited for a comment but none was forthcoming. He indicated the cardboard warning.

"We don't like this sort of thing. We don't find it at all funny. In a place like this where there are no teen-agers, no crackpots, no drunks, except occasionally at the inn, and no drug addicts, the possibility of misplaced humor has to be counted out.

"And in your case, with your husband just murdered, we don't like it at all. We'll see what we can make of this thing, though the chances are we won't find anything. But so far as you are concerned, I urge you most emphatically to go back to New York and stay there until we can smoke out this joker. Will you do that, Mrs.—Miss Edwards?"

"I'll take tomorrow's plane and I'll stay there until it is safe for me to come back," she agreed.

"Good. That's a big relief."

"But I might remind you that my husband was not killed here at the lake; he was thrown out of a window in New York."

There was a curious flicker in the trooper's eyes. "You didn't see anyone tonight?" He looked from Janice to Bertie.

"No one."

He spoke to Bertie. "Now, when you heard the crash, how long was it before you left your room to investigate?"

Bertie thought about it, weighing his words carefully. "Well, I was sound asleep. It took me a minute to get awake and realize what had awakened me. Then I had a kind of discussion with my wife, who didn't want me to go downstairs. You know how women are. Might have been three or four minutes."

"And when you went out of your room, where was Miss Edwards?"

"She was just coming out of her room and I asked her to wait until I investigated."

The trooper turned back to Janice. "Ever get any threats in New York?"

She shook her head.

"Your husband's death must have been a big shock to you. Just married, weren't you? And he'd come back that morning, took you to lunch, and then got called away. Have I got it right?"

She nodded.

"Uh-huh. So I guess you were mighty excited on Friday.

You went home after lunch to wait for your husband. Right?"

"No, I didn't know how long he would be. I went to the office, but my boss said to go home."

"Anyone see you go home?"

She shook her head.

"And then what?"

"I waited."

"I see," What he saw was blindingly clear to Janice.

"You don't believe me," she accused him. "You think— why, you think I killed my husband. You think I wrote that warning note to myself."

"Now have I said anything like that?" He smiled engagingly at her, but he met her unwavering stare steadily. "No law against thinking, is there, Mrs.—Miss Edwards?"

"None at all." She got up and the two men rose. "I think you ought to inform Lieutenant Carrigan of what happened up here. He's the New York man in charge of the murder of my husband."

"Now that's an idea," he said jovially. He looked at the revolver beside Bertie's hand. "Do you have a license for that?"

"The gun belonged to Mr. Ransome. He wanted me to have it for protection."

"Keep it loaded?"

"Oh, they are all loaded."

"All?" At his startled question Bertie led the way to the room Janice had referred to as an arsenal. The two troopers stood staring at the walls disbelief. Then the older man said, "Do you keep this room locked?"

Bertie shook his head. "We don't even lock the doors here."

"But, my God, anyone—" And Janice recalled that Strunski had availed himself of open doors to help himself to a revolver—a revolver which was still in Fritz's possession. "Miss Edwards, I don't know what you want with this stuff—"

"I don't want it at all," she said promptly. "It belonged to my stepfather and I haven't had time to dispose of it."

"I suggest that you get it touch with a local gunsmith and sell it at once. Meantime keep this room locked."

"Attend to it, will you?" Janice said, and Bertie agreed.

When the car door has slammed and the police car had rolled away, Janice said to Bertie, "They think I did it myself, you know," and without waiting for a reply she went upstairs. About the only advantage of that night's work was that in the excitement she had completely forgotten her headache.

II

Again it was noon before Janice awakened. For a long time she lay dozing, her thoughts drifting idly, and then the events of the night before rushed on her. When she had bathed and dressed, she went downstairs.

Mrs. Bertie came out of the kitchen exclaiming distressfully, "Why didn't you ring? I'd have brought you a tray."

"It's too nice a day to stay in bed."

"John's still sleeping, but then he never went to bed until daylight, when he was sure no one would be coming back. What goings-on at the lake, where nothing ever happens! There hasn't been anything wrong here since poor Mr. Nichols committed suicide and, if you ask me, that was a blessing in disguise. I've heard more than one person say he never would have made good."

When Janice had finished breakfast and looked out at the brilliant sky, she was tempted to take a walk and then, for the first time, the reality of the warning struck her.

She was sitting on the porch, unwilling to admit to herself that she was afraid to venture off it, pretending that she was merely lazy, enjoying a sleepy Sunday afternoon, when she heard the footsteps. Oh, not Thomas, she thought. Don't let it be Thomas. But it was not like his slow, heavy, deliberate tread. These steps were light and swift. And then Sonia came in sight, pushed open the screen door, and stood looking down at Janice as she lay on the long chair.

"I have only a few minutes," she said breathlessly. "I left

Vladimir conferring with Golschmann, and the rest of the party is busy, playing tennis or swimming, and I thought I'd just run over—" She came to a stop, checked by the ironic light in Janice's eyes.

"Sit down, Sonia, and stop dithering."

"I can't stay long. I just wanted—I had to know— Look, Janice, for God's sake, just what happened last night?"

For a moment Janice's face reflected her bewilderment and then she laughed. In the confusion of the housebreaking, the state police's patent disbelief of her story, the warning that she was to leave the lake, she had forgotten all about Strunski's attempt to shoot Sonia and her current admirer.

"Mr. Fitzgerald and I were getting a little fresh air before the trios started. Then, as you know, we practically ran into you with the actor and Vladimir standing there with a gun in his hand."

Sonia gave a whimpering cry. "I knew at the time it was risky," she admitted. "Vladimir could easily have been coming out for a cigarette or something. But he's never seemed to mind before. Janice, would he really—?"

Janice shrugged. "I don't know. It was loaded."

Sonia shivered. "And then what happened? I was so startled—I just stood there, rooted."

"Fitz jumped him and knocked his wrist so that he dropped the gun."

"I wouldn't have thought Vladimir cared that much," Sonia admitted. "I can't get him to say a word. He hasn't spoken to me since then, except in front of our guests, of course. I can't make him listen to reason. Do you think he'll get over it?"

"Actually," Janice said tartly, "I think he was much more concerned about whether Fitz had injured his wrist. I think it was just dramatics with him, but maybe not. Now and then I've wondered whether he wasn't about out of patience. Why do you go on playing the fool, Sonia? Why don't you give the poor man a break? He's given you the kind of life you like, the kind of friends you enjoy, and, God knows, enough rope."

"I never thought before there was any risk. A few kisses, a little mild flirtation—after all, I'm thirty-five, and a woman has to make hay while she can."

"You're forty," Janice reminded her, "and when you say a few kisses—" Her eyes rested on the jade ring.

Once more color rose in a scorching flame over Sonia's face and throat. "How did you know?"

"Bronze hairpins in my bed. A note on Bob's calendar about jade looking well with red. As it does," she added politely.

Without a word Sonia removed the ring and held it out to her. Janice shook her head.

"It never belonged to me. Just as Bob never belonged to me. You're welcome to it. I'll never want to wear it."

Sonia thrust it back on her finger awkwardly. "Well, thanks. I've got to get back to the inn. Golschmann wants to get in some bridge before the plane goes back. Be seeing you."

Janice heard her voice before she disappeared in the woods, so she was not surprised when Fitz came sauntering around and walked up on the porch.

"Apparently," he said pleasantly, as he perched on the porch railing, "our Hester has not been strangled by her long-suffering husband. I must say she wears her A's with a difference." He looked searchingly at her. "Everything okay?"

Janice told him about the forced window and the warning she had received and the belief of the state police that she had staged the whole thing herself. "As a red herring to convince the police that I did not murder Bob."

It was some time before he made any comment, then he said, "I wish to God you'd clear out."

"I'm going back on the afternoon plane, and this time I'll stay. Anyhow, I found out what I came for."

"I know. With the elimination of Lou Nichols from suspicion, you are left with a choice between Dave and me. Tell me, Janice, which of us do you believe left that warning for you last night?"

"Oh, don't be ridiculous."

"I see. Then there is someone else somewhere who might be involved?" The tone of detachment had altered. He took an involuntary step toward her, his hands out.

And the screen door of the porch crashed against the side of the house as Thomas came barging in. He looked from Janice to Fitz, his body seeming to quiver with rage. Fitz slid off the railing, balancing lightly as though ready to dive forward.

"Are you out of your mind, Janice?" Thomas said, his voice shaking. "Encouraging this man within a few days of your husband's murder? Don't you give a damn about what people will think? What's got into you?" He charged toward her and somehow Fitz was between them.

"What business is this of yours?" Thomas demanded.

"Or of yours, when it comes to that?" Fitz replied, his voice lazy, his eyes alert.

"It's any man but me, isn't it?" Thomas said harshly. "Any man. That bastard Maxwell. Then McClintock. Now it's this fellow. Sneaking off from the party with him last night. I'm ashamed of you, Janice. Do you know what you are? You—"

"Okay. You've spoken your piece." Fitz moved slowly, step by step, forcing Thomas backward until he was outside the porch. Then he slammed and locked the screen.

For a moment Thomas stood looking helplessly from one to the other and then he went down the steps and along the path at a shambling run.

SIXTEEN

VLADIMIR STRUNSKI was among those boarding the plane for New York. When he caught sight of him the musical comedy star looked so alarmed that Janice was tempted to laugh, as he could have made two of the other man. But Strunski ignored him. To Janice's surprise he buttonholed Fitz and said with a grim smile, "Last night I did not thank you for interfering. At that time I was not in a mood to be grateful. But I've had time to think it over and I have decided that a lawyer is more efficient than a gun in these cases and the result is just as final."

So Sonia had been wrong about his passive endurance. But had he, could he conceivably have, killed Bob if he knew of Sonia's affair with him?

Janice found herself being rather sorry for Sonia. What right had she to expect Sonia to be satisfied with her lot when Janice's own conduct could hardly have stood up to scrutiny? And Sonia, without Vladimir's backing and the position he provided for her, would be nothing at all, just another divorcée on the prowl, trying to build a precarious social world for herself.

Hal Striechen slid into the seat beside Janice. "Look, I've got to talk to you. I've got to explain about the whole business."

"But you did explain; you told me the cop couldn't take a joke."

"Oh, I admit I played a dirty trick on you but, hell, I was broke and that was the only way in sight to pick up a few bucks or at least get back what I had lost. I don't suppose you can see it from my viewpoint."

"No," she admitted, "I can't. Has it ever occurred to you to look for a job?"

He didn't bother to answer that. "Wasn't it Becky Sharp who said that anyone could be good on five thousand a year? And God knows," he added virtuously, "I wouldn't have done it at any price if I had known what was going to happen."

"It's nice to know you stop short of murder to protect your easy life."

Hal did not have a thin skin. "You'll let bygones be bygones, won't you? That is, you aren't going to get me kicked out of my rooms at the inn?"

She laughed. "I won't interfere with the management. That is up to them."

"Well, thanks a lot." He moved away to sit beside the actor. You never know when you'll make a useful contact and as long as he had his rooms at the inn he had a built-in way of providing hospitality. Janice, understanding his thought processes, grinned to herself. It would take more than Hal Streichen's offer of hospitality to lure the actor back to the inn. He would probably dream of irate husbands for a long time.

Janice saw that Thomas was eyeing the seat beside her, but before he could take it, Fitz had slipped into it. "My idea of giving you a wide berth doesn't seem to have worked out very well, but I'll be more comfortable sitting beside you than leaving you to your fiery friend Nichols."

"Fiery is a queer word to apply to plodding Thomas."

"That man is dangerous," Fitz told her quietly. "Have you heard anything further from the state police?"

She shook her head.

"Did you tell them that wasn't the first warning you had received? That Nichols had told you to stay away?"

"No, I didn't tell him about Thomas's warning. Or Dave's."

He looked at her thoughtfully. "Apparently Madame Strunski miscalculated. Her husband is going to sue for a divorce."

"I heard him." Her head dropped against his shoulder and she slept. She did not awaken until he fumbled with her seat belt.

"Here we are," he said cheerfully, steered her off the plane and hailed a taxi. He gave her address and climbed in after her.

"You needn't bother," she mumbled, still half asleep.

"No bother. Just want to make sure you are safe for the night."

She was awake then. "You mean that warning? But it applied only to the lake."

"Sure," he said. "Sure." But he followed her into the building, into the automatic elevator. There was no operator, even at night? The reception desk was around the corner, out of sight? He didn't like it.

She fumbled for her key and opened the door. When she had switched on lights, Fitz looked around him appraisingly. "Wait here."

"If you are trying to scare me, you are making a good job of it," Janice told him resentfully.

"Better safe than sorry." He went swiftly through the rooms—bedrooms, bathroom, dining room, kitchen and pantry, Janice following close at his heels, afraid to be left alone. "This place is really terrific, Janice. How about the terrace?" When she had switched on the artificial moonlight, they went out together, paying little attention to the view, looking at and around furniture and potted trees and bushes. When Fitz went around the corner, he shoved her behind him.

"But what are you really afraid of?" she demanded. "No one can get in."

"What happened to Maxwell's keys?"

"I don't know. I never thought about it."

"But he had a key to this apartment?"

"Oh, yes, of course."

"So there's a key floating around somewhere and probably in the hands of the murderer. I don't like this, Janice."

"You are making my blood run cold. And if it is any satisfaction to you, there are two missing keys." She explained having lost one a few weeks earlier. "I suppose, after all, someone did get in here to search Bob's things. At least that is what the police believe."

"Have a new lock put on in the morning, the first thing you do," Fitz said urgently, "and get a chain for the door. So far as I can make out, anyone can get in and out of this building without being observed. I don't like it a bit. Well, good night."

"Fitz?"

He came back and caught her in his arms, rocking her, holding her close, kissing her hair, her cheek, her throat, her mouth. Then he released her. "Damn it, I don't want to leave you, but I've got to. As things are, my staying here would bring police suspicions on us."

"Why on earth?"

"A motive for killing Maxwell."

"It's too late for that. They already suspect me."

"Look here." He showed her how to hook a chair under the knob of the door. "Do that tonight. Remember. And change the lock in the morning."

"Fitz," she said in a small, shaken voice, "will you kiss me good night?"

"I will not," he said grimly. "One more kiss and we'll both be lost."

"I believe you're afraid."

"I am afraid. To be blunt about it, I'm scared as hell."

II

In the night something new was added. As though she hadn't enough to bear, Janice thought, she was awakened by lancing, pulsing, throbbing pain in her jaw. For the rest of the night she kept filling an icebag, but it was small alleviation for the torment of an abscessed tooth. As soon as she could get hold of her dentist, she went to his office, her face badly swollen, and almost beside herself with pain.

So it was almost noon by the time Lieutenant Carrigan was able to reach her and it was late afternoon when he finally arrived with his tactiturn sergeant.

"Sorry to keep you waiting," the lieutenant said as he sat down on the terrace. "It's been one of those days. Mostly telephone calls and paper work, but it all has to be done. Well, now, just what happened up at your lake? I had quite a talk with the state police up there. What's all this about a housekeeper and a warning?" He listened noncommittally to Janice's account. "Do you have any ideas as to the identity of this joker?"

"The state police have ideas. They suspect I did it myself."

This obviously came as no surprise to the lieutenant. "What took you up there this weekend?"

"I wanted to see Lou Nichols and find out what condition he was in. He is the one with the strongest motive for killing Bob. But he couldn't have done it, Lieutenant. His brain has been hopelessly damaged. He is like a child. So that is out."

"We've checked on everyone in Maxwell's address book, both business and personal. Incidentally," and a tired grin flickered across the lieutenant's mouth, "we found the writer of that incendiary letter. She seems to have consoled herself in a hurry." His eyes rested on her face. "Some women do, you know."

Janice raised a casual eyebrow and met his look steadily, but she was aware that her color had risen.

Carrigan went on more briskly. "Oh, we found the writer of that blackmailing letter. He knew about Maxwell's contacts with the Communists, no doubt about it, but now Maxwell is dead and there are no golden eggs to be hatched, he isn't talking. Got a record, too, for attempted blackmail. Not a nice piece of goods. I hated to have to let him go."

He finished the iced coffee Janice had served, looked out

appreciatively at the view from the terrace. "Not that I should sit here," he admitted, "with those roses around. I'm allergic to roses. But for a few minutes of this view it's worth risking the kind of hay fever I get."

Someone else, Janice recalled, was allergic to roses, but she couldn't recall who it was and in any case it didn't seem important.

Just as Janice expected the policeman to leave, Carrigan said in that misleadingly casual manner of his, "Now, just for the record, Miss Edwards, let's take the whole thing from the beginning."

"Beginning where?"

"Let's start with your first meeting with Maxwell through this," he looked at notes, "Hal Streichen, and go on from there. Everything, please. Don't worry about repeating yourself."

Painstakingly Janice described meeting Bob on the plane, the evenings she had spent with him, their decision to be married privately without announcing it, the alibi that he had set up for the Atlantic City convention and the probability that he had spent that time driving to the Adirondacks to get a look at Lou—"and that would explain why he looked so relaxed when he came back, Lieutenant. If he saw Lou, he knew he had nothing to fear from him."

Once more she related how Bob had telephoned, presumably from a bus station in Atlantic City, the appointment that was made, the lunch at the Gotham broken up by the telephone call that had lured him to his death from the hotel room of M. Canning.

"So there we are," Carrigan said slowly. "We always come back to it, don't we? Only three people knew about that lunch at the Gotham: Mr. McClintock, Mr. Fitzgerald, and you. And not one of you has an alibi."

"There was someone at the office door when I was talking to Bob."

"Oh, yes. The little man who wasn't there."

As Janice stirred indignantly, he said, "Look, Miss Edwards, I'm trying to give you every possible break, whether you believe me or not. In fact, I am giving you a break. But just be reasonable. Where is your proof that someone listened to that telephone call and that the same person rushed off to set a trap for Maxwell?"

"It could have happened," she said stubbornly. "And the door opened. Someone listened."

"The door might have been blown open by a draft."

She gave up in despair. "I don't see how you could possibly suspect me of making that call. Why, I was sitting right there at the table in plain sight when Bob was paged."

"Telephone calls can be arranged."

"I suppose they can be. But we were just married and we—at least I was in love. So why?"

"So now we come down to why. Mr. McClintock apparently had a motive. He hated Maxwell because he had betrayed a fellow prisoner. Now with Mr. Fitzgerald we have a different why. He's interested in you, but whether," Carrigan said bluntly, "it's you or your money, I don't know. I wouldn't bet a dime on it either way."

"Well, that's frank, at least."

"Sometimes it clears the air to be frank. What I do know is that Fitzgerald, like a fool, went up to your lake with you this weekend."

"He didn't go because of me. Dave sent for him. He was horribly upset because the police had been questioning him."

"And then Fitzgerald escorted you home, came up here with you, but didn't stay very long."

"Are you having me followed Lieutenant?"

"For your own protection. I should think, in the light of that anonymous warning, it would give you a feeling of security."

"What that your intention?" It was a rhetorical question. She did not expect a reply. Obviously he believed that she had no reason to be afraid of that warning. Just as obviously Fitz had sound reason for being afraid. The police were watching his every move.

The lieutenant with a final look at the view—it was twilight and the city lights were having their usual magical effect—got up to leave and this time he did not offer to shake hands.

At the door Janice said quickly, "I've remembered something that happened Saturday night." She described Fitz knocking the gun out of Strunski's hand when the latter confronted his wife and the actor. Later he had taken the plane to New York, telling Fitz he was going to consult a lawyer about a divorce. "So if—" Janice's voice trailed off uncertainly.

"If this man Strunski was mad enough to try to shoot his rival, he might have been mad enough to try to get rid of Maxwell. Is that what you are suggesting?"

"Well—" Janice battled with temptation. Then she shook her head. "I don't honestly believe he could," she admitted.

For the first time the lieutenant's smile was altogether friendly. Then it faded. "Where did he get the gun?"

"From my house. There's a room like an arsenal with rifles, shotguns, handguns, anything you can think of. My stepfather collected them."

"Locked away, of course."

She shook her head. "I know it was criminally careless, but nothing ever happened before. I left instructions with my houseman to pack them all up and sell them to a local gunsmith."

SEVENTEEN

WHEN THE POLICEMEN had gone, Janice went impulsively to the telephone and dialed Fitz's number. And then, without waiting for a reply, she broke the connection, staring blankly at the wall. Fitz had been honest with her. He had told her that he was afraid. That was why he had left her in such haste the night before. When she was with him, there was no doubt in her mind as to his trustworthiness, his unshakable integrity. But at a distance she remembered only that he had displayed no personal interest in her until after he knew of her inheritance, and that she had been mistaken, totally and blindly mistaken, in Bob.

By this time the novocaine had worn off but the taste of disinfectant in her mouth made her slightly sick and she wanted no food, though she had eaten no lunch because of her sore mouth.

She undressed, piled pillows high on her bed, found the bottle of pain killer she had brought down from the lake and placed it on her bedside table with a teaspoon. According to the directions she could take one every four hours. She had been given the prescription months before when she had suffered from a lame back, and had forgotten about it until her severe headaches began. Somewhat to her surprise she found it on the front of a shelf in her medicine cabinet and not among other unused medicines.

Awkwardly she poured into the spoon and most of the medicine spilled on the bed and the carpet leaving only a few drops. She swallowed them but it was too much trouble to unscrew the cap of the bottle again. So she lay back on the bed and closed her eyes.

Something bothered her, something lurking in the back of her mind, something she had forgotten. Oh, of course, new locks and a chain for the door. That day she had thought only of the toothache but she would take care of the locks in the morning. Meanwhile she ought to hook a chair under the doorknob. Before she could do so the discomfort of which she had been increasingly aware, a faint stirring of nausea, became acute and could not be ignored. She got out of bed.

This was ridiculous. She was lurching like a drunken man and the floor rose and fell under her feet like the deck of a ship. Probably it was a result of the extraction, the novocaine, and a lack of food.

She was violently sick, the heavy vomiting leaving her so weak that she found it difficult to maintain her balance, but by holding one hand against the wall she could steady herself as she wove her way back to bed.

That was when she heard the slow, heavy footsteps in the living room Startled, she called out, "Who is there?"

There was no answer, but the steps halted. She stood leaning against the wall, holding her breath, her heart making such a tumult that she felt it would betray her. In the living room someone was listening as she was listening. She was in danger and she must think clearly, but her thoughts swirled, murky, incoherent, like the bad dreams that had followed Bob's death, except that this was real.

It would do no good to call for help; no one could hear her from the penthouse. But if she could get to the telephone which was in the foyer beside the door, she could call the police. The problem was that she would have to cross the dark living room to reach it, and in the living room someone waited for her to make a move.

There was no creaking of the floor because the building was too well built and the carpeting was deep and thick.

Whoever waited in the dark was moving quietly now, footsteps muffled. Janice crept closer to the door. Anything was better than being trapped in this room where there was noplace to run. If only she had one of the dozens of guns at Peaceful Haven, but there was nothing which could serve as a weapon or even as protection.

It had never occurred to her to have a key to the bedroom doors in the apartment. There was no way she could barricade herself. Again she stood, holding her breath, straining to hear. But the only sounds that reached her were the familiar ones: muted roar of traffic, sirens of police and fire and ambulance, the whistle of the doorman across the street signaling for a taxi.

A police whistle! Tomorrow she would try to buy one. That would be some sort of protection. Next time she would be better prepared.

If there was a next time.

Noiselessly she eased open the door. The living room, like her bedroom, was dimly lighted by the glow of the city itself. She could make out the outlines of furniture and the long line of pale oblongs that were the windows opening on the terrace. At the edge of her vision something moved, but when she turned her head swiftly, she could make out no one in the shadowy room.

Then the hem of her nightgown was stirred by a draft. The door to the terrace had been opened. That meant, didn't it, that the intruder had gone out on the terrace so there was a chance, slim but the only chance she had, that she could reach the telephone and ask for help.

She looked into the big, menacing room and thought, *I can't do it. I can't.* But she had no choice. In satin slippers her feet made no sound as she groped her way as swiftly as possible into the darkened room. It was a footstool that, literally, was her downfall. She stumbled over it and lost her balance. The noise sounded like a thunderclap.

And then there was movement behind her. She turned to face the danger and screamed as the spray touched her face, flung up a hand to shield her eyes as she staggered away, out of range.

Someone gripped her arm and propelled her, recoiling and blinded, across the room, while a low muttering went on and on. Then they were on the terrace, moving toward the stone railing, and still Janice could not cry out, could not see, could not defend herself, already weakened by that acute attack of nausea.

People always thought it could never happen to them. She could not imagine her own death. And to die like this, horribly, terrifyingly, and pointlessly. What good could her death do to anyone? It's going to happen to me, she thought. It is happening now. She was defenseless against the fierce strength of the hand that had driven her against the stone railing. She could go no further. It was like one of those nightmares when one's legs refuse to move, when one cannot cry out. But this was real. This was real!

The hand released its cruel grip of her arm but before she could move, her ankles were seized and someone had begun to lift her.

As her feet felt the ground, she was aware of such terror as she had never before conceived of. Like Bob, she thought. Like Bob. I'm going to die. I'm going to fall. Oh, God, don't let it happen. Don't let it happen. Please. Please. Don't let—

Her body in its soft, silky gown slid easily up the railing. Her head was above it, then her shoulders, then—
Her arms flailed, groping at air, groping at nothing.

II

There were shouts and pounding feet. The hideous inexorable propelling of her helpless body over the railing was checked. The grasp on her ankles was relaxed and strong hands seized her by the waist. And then she screamed—wildly, shrilly.

Thomas shouted, "Don't hurt her. I warn you. Don't hurt her."

Through half-open glazed eyes she became aware that Thomas was lifting her, not over the railing but away from it, lifting her into safety. And on the floor of the terrace someone was struggling fiercely with Fitz.

Fitz? That was the ultimate horror. If it was Fitz who had tried to kill her, then nothing mattered at all. She was grateful for the merciful blackness into which she sank.

She was unconscious only a few seconds and then she choked as Thomas held a glass to her lips and made her swallow. The fiery brandy stung her throat but her heart steadied and she looked up. Thomas was kneeling beside her, raising her head on his arm, his face white and drawn.

"Oh, Janice," he said over and over. "Oh, Janice."

And then the apartment door was flung back on its hinges and two policemen plunged into the room. One of them ran to the two people who thrashed on the floor; the other came to bend over Janice who, aware of his expression, realized that the gown she was wearing was diaphanous.

She put aside the glass Thomas was holding. "I'm not hurt." She clutched at the policeman's sleeve. "He nearly killed me, Officer. He was trying to push me off the terrace. I was half over the railing." Long shudders ran down her body.

"This guy?" His expression was ugly.

"No, this is a friend who saved me." She tried to pull the nightgown over her.

The policeman picked her up and carried her into her room. "You'll be all right now, miss. Nothing to worry about. We have it under control and we'll sort it out." As voices were raised on the terrace, he left her and ran back.

With the arrival of the police there was nothing to fear. Janice pulled on a robe, tied the belt, and staggered to the door. She heard Thomas's voice raised in a shout of anger, saw the two policemen bending over a crouching figure on the terrace floor, saw Fitz get to his feet, wiping blood from his face.

"Don't hurt her," Thomas shouted. And then he knelt beside the frenzied woman who was being restrained by the two policemen who were trying to prevent her from hurting herself.

"Mother! Take it easy. Everything is all right. Don't you know me, Mother? It's Thomas."

And Grace Nichols crumpled in a heap on the floor, sobbing.

Leaving her to the care of her son, one of the policemen went to Fitz, whose face had been clawed, his collar ripped away, a sleeve torn. "Better see a doctor. You look as though you had tangled with a buzz saw."

"That's the way I feel. She's demented, you know. You'll have to watch yourself. She's incredibly strong."

"What was it all about? We got a squeal from some people who were on a terrace across the street. They thought someone was being pushed off the railing here—"

"That's what nearly happened."

"How did you get here?"

"I'll tell you the whole thing later."

As Grace began to shout, the policeman ran to help his partner. In a moment he came back, got names and addresses, said they would be called for questioning, and went to help drag Grace away, followed by Thomas.

"The lady was saved by seconds," the younger of the two men said to Fitz as the little procession went out of the apartment. "God, what a thing!"

There was silence in the living room after the men had left. Janice sat on the couch, shaking with a chill in spite of the rope wrapped around her, her eyes blank with shock. But at least some of the paralysis had gone from her face and, though her eyes stung, she could see.

Fitz went out on the terrace, saw the shambles from that violent tussle with the madwoman, and came back wiping his head. He locked the terrace door.

Feeling like a zombie, Janice tried to bring order out of the chaos in her mind, to understand what had happened, and why it had happened. But the only thing that was clear was that Fitz was all right. *Fitz was all right.*

Vividly she remembered the helpless feeling when her feet had left the ground, when her body had begun to slide up the railing, over— She gave a little whimper of fear.

Fitz called, "I'm coming, darling. Just a minute."

And then he was there with a bowl of hot soup. "Drink all of it. You're in shock. You need warmth and you need something to steady you."

Her fingers touched her face. "What happened? What's wrong with my face?"

"A tear-gas spray. One of the cops found it on the terrace. One of those gadgets women buy to carry in their handbags in case of mugging. There's no permanent damage. Just a kind of facial paralysis that wears off in a comparatively short time."

"A tear-gas spray. One of Lou's practical jokes. He got jailed for that once. So that is how it was possible for a big man to be overpowered by a woman."

"That's how."

"But Grace! I can't understand how she got in here."

"We'll know in time," he told her. "And," he added reprovingly, "if you'd remembered about changing the locks she couldn't have got in."

"And Thomas came too! Does that mean he knew about his mother all the time?"

"He knew. Poor devil. He saved you, Janice. No, drink that, all of it."

"I can't. It's boiling."

"Do as you are told."

When she had obediently drunk all the soup she said, "Is the nightmare over now?"

"For you it's all over," he assured her. He picked her up and carried her into her room, put her on the bed and pulled a sheet over her. Then he noticed the sticky substance on the sheet and on the floor. "What's that?"

"A pain killer I brought down from the lake but I spilled most of it."

Fitz picked up the bottle, unscrewed the cap, smelled it, moistened the top of his finger with it and tasted it cautiously.

"Where did you get this?"

She told him. Then she recalled her surprise at finding the bottle in plain sight. "And I'd taken most of it, as I remembered, but the bottle was nearly full. Fitz! Is there something wrong? I got only a few drops."

"That's why you are alive," Fitz told her. "Grace must have put the stuff in your bottle. But how could she have got hold of poison?"

"Her husband killed himself with some stuff. The police didn't make public what it was. They don't, you know, because it gives people ideas."

Fitz wrapped the bottle carefully and slipped it in his pocket.

"Where are you going?" she asked in a panic.

"Living room. I'll sleep on the couch tonight, though nothing more will happen. Call me if you are frightened. But you'll have to make an honest man of me, you understand."

Janice did not answer. She was asleep.

EIGHTEEN

FITZ WAS GONE when Janice awakened the next morning. In a way she was glad. She could not have coped even with Fitz in her condition. The combination of tooth extraction, poison, and a hair's breadth escape from death had left her in a state of almost total exhaustion.

Without daring to go out, she peered at the terrace where overturned chairs and small tables and trampled bushes were a reminder of that terrible struggle between Fitz and the madwoman.

For mad was the operative word, Lieutenant Carrigan explained when he called that afternoon. He came in waving a handkerchief like a white flag.

"Okay. Say it. Say anything you like. I'll eat all my words." He tried to speak lightly but he was appalled when he saw her. The girl looked like walking death, and after she had described as clearly as she could what had happened, as far as she could piece it together, he marveled at the sheer luck that had saved her at the eleventh hour.

"Mr. Fitzgerald gave me that bottle and, after we'd had it analyzed, we checked it with the M.D. who prescribed a pain killer for you. He nearly had a fit. Anyhow, we found Mrs. Nichols's prints on it. Not that it matters. She readily admitted putting the stuff in your medicine bottle. She tried everything, didn't she? Tear gas, poison, a hammer. And she sure has a predilection for open windows and high places. At least, where she is going there will be bars she can't push anyone through."

"But why me? I think I can understand in a way about Bob. When she knew what he had done to the son she has always adored she must have wanted to kill him."

"But the joker in the pack is that she didn't know. She doesn't know now. Nichols was stunned when I told him this morning that Maxwell had been responsible for his brother's tragedy. No, Mrs. Nichols had just one fixed idea. You were to marry her son because she felt sure you'd be rich some day and give him an easy life. Well, when he came home, she saw just as much of his condition as she was willing to believe. He was a sick man who needed care and you were the one who ought to provide it. When she had to acknowledge the permanent damage to his brain, you were to be a compensation for all his sufferings. You could cushion the rest of his life. I think by that time she had begun to blame you for what had happened to him."

"But why did the army release him in that condition?"

"It was an experiment. He's like a small child and when things go wrong, he cries for his mother. A couple of the head-shrinkers thought it might help him to be with her. Of course, it didn't work out. He'll be institutionalized for life and so will his mother."

"Poor Thomas."

"In one way, of course. But look at the other side of the coin, Miss Edwards," Carrigan said, half amused that this woman who looked like death itself after her long ordeal was more perturbed about the unhappiness of someone else. "He's a free man now and, if you ask me, for the first time in his life."

As he reached for his hat, Janice, afraid to be alone, said quickly, "Tell me the rest of it."

"Are you sure you want all this?"

"I'm sure."

"Well, a week ago Tuesday, Mrs. Nichols came to New

York with the pretext of buying civilian clothes for Lou. Actually she came straight up here to your apartment."

"How could she get in?"

"You had once dropped a key in her cottage, at least that is the way her son Thomas figures it. Anyhow, she took a good look around, found Maxwell's clothes and those letters and realized that you must be married to one Robert Maxwell. She looked the place over and went out on the terrace. Like me, she is allergic to roses and she got this attack of sinus. When she ran out of tissues, she took some of your handkerchiefs."

As Janice gave a startled exclamation, he nodded.

"Later Thomas found them neatly laundered in a drawer of her dresser, where he also found Maxwell's papers and the rest of the stuff he had in his pockets. And by then he already knew because when the news hit the papers with the name of M. Canning, he recognized it as his grandmother's maiden name."

Unexpectedly Janice laughed. "I can't help wondering how Grace Nichols and Sonia Strunski avoided meeting each other here on Tuesday."

The lieutenant shrugged. Janice seemed to be coming out of it, though she was still too weak to walk without support.

"The possibility of you marrying another man came as a terrible shock to Mrs. Nichols, who had come to believe that it was your function to make life pleasant not only for her son but for her as well, as she had no intention of being separated from him. My guess is that she began to work out various plans to eliminate Maxwell that day. Anyhow, she went back to New York on Friday without informing Thomas of her intentions. He was stunned when he saw her on the homebound plane. She offered no explanation but she acted, he thought, strange, excited, almost triumphant. Apparently when she left the cottage, she had locked Lou in his room.

"Well, she had made up her mind that Maxwell was to die. She brought with her one of Lou's tear-gas sprays and, in a big handbag, she carried a hammer from the cottage. She went straight to your office. God knows what she had in mind, because by then she must have been well around the bend, but apparently she wanted to find out from you where Maxwell was. She had no idea of the need for concealment."

For the first time Janice was alert. "Then she was the one who opened the office door but never came in."

Carrigan nodded and again he pulled out his white handkerchief and waved it. "Yes, she was the one who opened the door and overheard your conversation over the telephone with Maxwell. I'm sorry about that, but you'll have to admit that it sounded far-fetched."

"Everything that has happened so far has sounded far-fetched," Janice admitted.

"I figured you were drawing a red herring across the path to take attention away from you, and the heat off Fitzgerald. Well, I was wrong about that. Anyhow, Mrs. Nichols had found out the main thing, which was where Maxwell would be at a certain time. So all she had to do was to set a trap. She went to the hotel, registered as M. Canning, and asked for a room high up so she could get a view." Janice shivered. "Then she waited until she could have Maxwell paged at the Gotham. According to what her son Thomas got out of her late last night she said, 'I know the truth about you and you can't get away with it.' What she meant, of course, was his secret marriage. What Maxwell thought she meant only he could tell. Heaven knows he had enough reasons to feel guilty on a score of charges."

Carrigan got up to walk to the windows and look out on the terrace. His face was grim when he came back. No wonder the woman sat there frozen.

"So," he went on, his voice cheerful, "Maxwell put on the disguise he still had in his pocket because he had just returned from the Adirondacks, where he had gone to look at Lou Nichols. This time he went to meet M. Canning and he must have been half crazy wondering who he was and what he wanted. Now he was on the verge of making his big haul." He saw Janice wince. Well, she might as well have the whole thing clear now. "Whatever he expected to find, it was a middle-aged woman. She told her son that as soon as Maxwell entered the room she used the tear-gas spray and while he was helpless and blinded she struck him with the hammer, killing him instantly. At least she must have done so, as there was only the one blow and the doctor says he was dead before he fell.

"She went through his pockets, took out everything, and then she hoisted him out of the window and went down in the elevator. She was one of the crowd that watched while he was picked up. She said it was very interesting. By then I think she had gone completely over the brink. But all Thomas knew on Friday night was that something was wrong with his mother and there was trouble with Lou, who had been left locked in all day and was crying his head off.

"Next day, what with the story about M. Canning, his mother's trip to New York, and her attitude, he was convinced that she had killed Maxwell. Everything he has done since then has been to keep you away from the lake and away from his mother."

"Poor Thomas," Janice said again.

"He told me it was hell."

"Is he the one who left that crude warning for me?"

Carrigan nodded. "Apparently he had done his best to persuade you to stay in New York. He was torn two ways, of course. He didn't want to betray his mother and he didn't want anything to happen to you. I got the impression that he cared a lot about what happened to you. It's curious, isn't it, that Mrs. Nichols should have destroyed Maxwell without knowing that he was the one who had destroyed her son. There's a kind of poetic justice in that, isn't there?"

"But she is dangerous, Lieutenant."

"Potentially dangerous, but she won't ever again be a danger to anyone." Again, as though drawn by some irrestible attraction, Carrigan went to look out at the terrace and the signs of the struggle. "Well, I guess that about covers it."

"Lieutenant, why did Grace try to kill me after Bob was dead?"

"Because you seemed to be friendly with this man McClintock and with Fitzgerald. People in the colony were talking about it, hoping you'd find someone to take Maxwell's place and give you a better break. And then there was her son Thomas. If Lou couldn't have you she was determined that no one would."

"I suppose it made a kind of sense to her. What brought Thomas to the penthouse just when—" Her throat closed and she began to shake.

"A Mrs. Peters called to tell him that Mrs. Nichols had taken their car about noon and had not returned it. Apparently Thomas had pocketed the keys to Lou's car and Mr. Peters was known to be careless about things like that. Mrs. Peters wasn't worried about her car but she was worried about Mrs. Nichols, who never left her son Lou for any length of time. She thought Thomas ought to know. Well, the poor devil didn't know what to do."

"Thomas," Janice admitted, "rarely does."

"He didn't want to call the police and involve his mother. But he knew the chances were that you were in danger. He got up here as fast as he could and he came as close to being too late that it makes my blood run cold."

Janice pushed herself farther back in her chair as though assuring herself that it was anchored to the floor, that she was safe. Her hands gripped the wooden arms. Her forehead was beaded with perspiration.

"It's all right," the lieutenant said loudly. "You're safe."

She opened her eyes and made herself relax. "I was just remembering. Go on. I'd rather know all of it now and get it over."

He watched her uneasily for a moment. He had not believed anyone could be much paler than she was, but every vestige of color had drained from her face.

"If you say so," he said reluctantly. "Where was I?

Well, the first person Thomas saw was Fitzgerald climbing out of a taxi. Apparently," and for the first time the lieutenant grinned, "they eyed each other like a couple of strange dogs. They both said, 'What are you doing here?' Then Thomas came out with it. 'I'm worried about Janice.' 'So am I,' Fitzgerald told him; 'I told her to have the locks changed on her door and I want to check.' And I must say you should have done that, Miss Edwards."

"I had to go to the dentist with an abscessed tooth. That was all I could think of."

"So that's why! I don't know of a better reason. Well, they went upstairs together and found the door of the apartment ajar, saw the terrace door open and—I guess you know more about all that than I do. They tore Mrs. Nichols away from you and she put up a terrific fight, biting, clawing, kicking. Fitzgerald tried to control her without hurting her or letting her hurt herself and he got mauled as though he had tangled with a wild cat, as, in a way, he did. And meanwhile someone in a terrace apartment across the street saw something of the fracas and called the police. Any questions?"

Janice shook her head. "I suppose I'll take it all in sometime. But I wonder if I'll ever sleep again without nightmares. I've decided not to keep this apartment. I'll be afraid to set foot on the terrace."

"I don't often give unsolicited advice," Carrigan said, "but I'd strongly advise you not to do that. If you run away from that fear it will be with you always. Stay and face it. Oh, go away for a while, by all means. But come back and look the thing in the face. It's the fears we bury that really bug us."

"I don't know where to go."

"Go back to your lake." He saw her expression. "It will be all right. Mrs. Nichols won't be there and her cottage will be empty. Mrs. Peters released poor Lou and I guess his room was a bit of a mess but that can be cleaned up. He has already been taken away by the authorities. And Mrs. Nichols won't stand trial. It's all right."

NINETEEN

SUMMER ENDED with a long, exhausting heat wave in September and then autumn performed its brief miracle of brilliant color, deep blue skies, crisp air. And when the maples and oaks and elms dropped their leaves, standing stark, people remembered to be grateful to the evergreens. The lake was too cold for water sports, the hunting season came and went, summer visitors relinquished their rooms at the inn, which slept most of the week, awakening to mild entertainment over the weekends. There were still enough guests to form bridge tables, but Vladimir Strunski had given his last party of the season.

And the cold weather came. Because of Mrs. Bertie's tireless care, Janice began to put on weight and her skin glowed with a healthy color. She walked in the woods for hours and came back with a robust appetite. She seemed the same except to the watchful eyes of the Berties, who knew that she was too quiet, too much alone.

She was living in an irrational agony of self-reproach. Because of her gullibility she had unleashed this horror. Bob was dead, she had so nearly died, both Lou and Grace Nichols had been condemned to a living death, poor Thomas had been stripped of everything he valued. The lieutenant had been right. Janice did not know people.

Now in the light of the tragedies her blunders had caused, she was afraid of people. She needed to steer clear of them.

Plans had been completed for expanding the colony, and as soon as the frost was out of the ground in the spring work would begin on clearing the land and building new cottages. As word of the project spread, tentative applications began to filter in. These Janice turned over to a committee she had appointed after long consultation with Vladimir Strunski, Jake Peters, and the Authors' League. She did not consult Fitz. Since the night when Grace had tried to kill her, she had not seen or heard from him.

She read publicity stories in the *Publishers Weekly* announcing the first list of Gamaliel Fitzgerald, which was to appear in the spring. There were several titles that were new to her and she wondered, in a flare of jealousy, who was working now as Fitz's assistant. The plan of a partnership she had put away with her other dreams and illusions.

So far, shut away from everyone, she had seen none of the people who lived at the lake, with the exception of a brief and painful interview with Thomas, who had come up to pack his mother's clothes. He had aged and his shoulders stooped as though he were an old man.

"I won't say goodbye. I won't try to say how sorry I am for—everything."

"There's nothing to say. I'm terribly sorry for you, Thomas."

"No, don't be. I think I can stand anything but your pity, Janice. I—" He turned to go. "Thank you for letting me leave Lou's car here. I'll come back for it later but right now, what with Mother's—hospitalization—and the cost of renting a garage for a car in New York, it's a break to be able to leave it here, if you are sure it is all right with you."

"Of course it's all right. Take as long as you like. We won't be ready for new people until next summer, you know. And if you'd like to keep the cottage—"

"Good God!" He gave her a horrified look and went down the steps, walking toward the inn where, for the last time, he would take the plane for New York.

Dave McClintock had been careful to stay out of the way and if he was in communication with Fitz, he gave no inkling of it. Helen and Jake Peters bided their time. When Janice wanted them they would be waiting, but she did not seem to want them now, to want anyone.

About one thing Carrigan had been right. Little by little, the nightmares were fading. Less and less often she dreamed that she was being forced over the railing, that she was falling into space.

Vladimir Strunski was the first to break through her self-imposed isolation, not for her sake, but because he wanted something and it did not occur to him to consider her wishes. He encountered her on a path through the woods.

"You never come near me," he complained.

"I'm not good company."

"I don't know what's wrong with you. Well, don't tell me if you don't want to. The thing is this, Janice: I want my cottage. I know this place is for artists in need, but I'm in need of peace and quiet, the kind I can get here in this isolated community. Let me buy the place and remodel it to suit myself. If you like, I'll pay for another cottage and its maintenance so some poor devil won't be defrauded of a place to work."

Janice considered for a moment. Strunski broke in, "After all, you know, I do lend prestige to this place."

She laughed at him. "All right, if it means so much to you, I'll let you buy it. But do you mean to live here alone?"

There was malice in his smile. "As you probably know, I consulted my lawyer. Then Sonia and I had a long talk; or rather I talked. I told her what I intended to do. I explained that I meant to make this my permanent home, leaving it only for recitals, concerts, and that sort of thing. I told her that she could stay here, on my terms, or we would divorce and she could be free to set up for herself elsewhere. I must say I expected it would take her longer than it did to make up her mind, but then I suppose she has fewer opportunities for philandering than she used to have. She decided that she would settle for what I could give her rather than live the precarious, drifting life of a divorcée. Sonia, though you may not credit it, is a very conventional woman. In her fashion, of course; in her fashion. But from now on it will be in my fashion."

As he was about to enter his studio, he turned back. "I'm preparing for my recital in February, probably my last personal appearance. I'll open the program with the Bach Toccata and Fugue in D Minor. Come hear me practice at any time. I always do better with an audience." He waved his hand and trotted off to his piano.

As though that meeting with Strunski had released something that had been captive in her, Janice went briskly toward the Peters's cottage. Jake was on a ladder fastening on storm windows. He waved a hammer at her cheerfully, as though he had seen her the day before. "Battening down the hatches," he called.

"Jake," Helen protested as she came out, bundled in an old coat, "what on earth are you doing?"

"Sewing us up for the winter."

"Jake," she wailed, "you forget. We're going to Arizona for the winter on that money Janice paid you. Oh, Janice," and she was as casual as though this were any meeting, "you can't imagine the effect of that sale. Jake has sold three more paintings for fabulous prices, simply outrageous. So we are running away from the cold this winter." She tucked her hand under Janice's arm. "Time for sherry. Come in and we'll have some clam chowder and eat it in front of the fire. It's nice on a day like this."

They sat in front of a noisily crackling fire and ate clam chowder while Jake and Helen talked lightly about their winter plans, not requiring any response, simply gathering Janice into their fold, into their warmth.

She found herself looking at the vivid Spanish lady on the wall and Jake followed her gaze. "You know, Helen," he said, "it's fantastic to see how little you've changed."

They were aroused by the roar of a motor and Helen went to the window. "We have so few cars here in the winter," she said, "that I always look out to see who is going past. Generally it is only an oil truck or the snowplow and sander. Good heavens, it's Thomas. Why, he's got Lou's sports car."

Around the curve of the road roared the little sports car. At the wheel sat Thomas, wearing a rakish red hunting cap. Seeing them, he flipped a careless hand and zoomed up an incline and out of sight.

"Exit Thomas," Jake said, "tasting the sweets of freedom. Long may he flourish." And then he felt it was safe to say, in a casual way, "Lou is getting fine care now and he seems to be happy. Helen was checking with the authorities a couple of weeks ago. And Grace has withdrawn so far into her unreal world that she, too, has found a refuge. So Thomas is free at last to build a life for himself and—"

"If you say 'All's well that ends well,' I will hit you," his wife threatened him.

He grinned at her. Abruptly he asked Janice, "How long are you going to go on hiding up here?"

"I suppose, in a way, that's what I have been doing. Licking my wounds."

"What are you afraid of?"

"Going back to that apartment, to that terrace."

"Going back alone, you mean." Jake ignored his wife's warning touch on his arm. "You remember that thing of Edna St. Vincent Millay's about—what was it?—something about the fear of the mustering years at our back, or some such thing, the shapes that seldom will attack:

> Two with a light who match their steps and sing;
> For one alone and lost, another thing.

That night, as though the whole colony had determined to break through her self-imposed isolation, Dave McClintock called. After a casual conversation he said, "Janice, I've finished the rough draft of my book."

"Oh, I'm so glad."

"Well, the thing is, it's a lonely and unsatisfactory business trying to celebrate all by myself. Let's go to the inn and dance. I'm not much good, but at the moment I think I could dance on the table."

She laughed and to her own surprise accepted. "I'll do that only if you promise to stay off the table. Shall I pick you up?"

"No, I'll meet you at the inn."

But it wasn't Dave McClintock who was waiting for her in the lounge. It was Fitz, looking taller than ever, watching for her in mingled eagerness and doubt. She came to a halt when she saw him and he stood waiting. So in the long run she went to him. He took her hands, looking deep into her eyes, and at what he saw in them his color returned and she was aware of how white he had been before.

"Let's have our cocktails here, shall we?" he said, and indicated one of the small tables set out in the lobby, each with its small bell for service. On the balcony a few strings played softly, part of the band to which they would dance later.

"Isn't this rather conspicuous?" she asked doubtfully.

"What are you afraid of, Janice? Of course, it's conspicuous. True, not more than three people here know who you are. I see the ubiquitous Hal. No, don't turn now, he is looking this way. He seems to have latched onto a septic female who spent the whole flight talking in a high-pitched voice about her collection of old jewelry." He added, "Dave isn't coming, you know."

"This was just a trap," she accused him, her eyes alight.

"A trap," he agreed. "How long are you going to stay here?"

"I don't know. There's nothing to keep me and yet I don't want to go back."

"If you don't want to live in the penthouse," he said, "we can find another apartment, or maybe a house in Westchester. But I object to Long Island because I need transportation. I've no objection to New Jersey." For all his light tone he watched her closely. Then he rang the bell and ordered a daiquiri for her and a martini for himself.

She could bear it no longer. "Why didn't you come? All this time and you didn't call or write or anything."

"I told you once before I didn't want any shadows between us. I had to wait for the shadows to fade. Have they?"

"I don't know."

"Shall I start househunting?"

"I wouldn't be afraid of the terrace if I didn't have to go there alone." Before he could speak, she rushed on, "Who has replaced me at the office?"

"No one could replace you. I have a woman with a face like a box of cereal who does typing and takes calls and ships out the impossible manuscripts."

"What about those Gothics?"

"They are piling up. They can't wait much longer."

"Fitz?"

"What is it, darling?"

"I was thinking—before all this happened—I'd like to go into partnership with you."

"One kind doesn't exclude the other, you know." He raised his glass and touched hers. Then he set it down and rushed back his chair. "Let's get out of here."

"Why?" she exclaimed in surprise.

"I want to kiss you."

"Not out of doors with the temperature down to fifteen degrees," she said firmly, though her color rose.

"There's no romance in women," he grumbled as he picked up his glass.

She laughed at him. "We've got all the time in the world." She gasped as she heard the echo of Bob's words, and then realized that they no longer hurt. "All the time in the world," she repeated confidently.

ON SALE WHEREVER PAPERBACKS ARE SOLD
— or use this coupon to order directly from the publisher.

REX STOUT

MORE BEST SELLING PAPERBACKS BY
ONE OF YOUR FAVORITE AUTHORS...

REX STOUT

ADVENTURES OF NERO WOLFE:

V4027	**BLACK ORCHIDS $1.25**
V4089	**FER-DE-LANCE $1.25**
V4143	**THE LEAGUE OF FRIGHTENED MEN $1.25**
V4158	**NOT QUITE DEAD ENOUGH $1.25**
V4138	**OVER MY DEAD BODY $1.25**
V4163	**THE RED BOX $1.25**
V4119	**THE RUBBER BAND $1.25**
V4134	**SOME BURIED CAESAR $1.25**
V4112	**TOO MANY COOKS $1.25**

OTHER MYSTERIES

V4065	**THE BROKEN VASE $1.25**
V4149	**THE HAND IN THE GLOVE $1.25**
V3173	**THE PRESIDENT VANISHES $1.25**
·V3875	**THE RED MENACE $1.25**
V3071	**RED THREADS $1.25**
V3083	**THE SOUND OF MURDER $1.25**

Send To: JOVE PUBLICATIONS, INC.
Harcourt Brace Jovanovich, Inc.
Dept. M.O., 757 Third Avenue, New York, N.Y. 10017

NAME _____

ADDRESS _____

CITY _____

STATE _____ ZIP _____

I enclose $_____, which includes the total price of all books ordered plus 50¢ per book postage and handling for the first book and 25¢ for each additional. If my total order is $10.00 or more, I understand that Jove Publications, Inc. will pay all postage and handling.

No COD's or stamps. Please allow three to four weeks for delivery. Prices subject to change.

NT-14

ON SALE WHEREVER PAPERBACKS ARE SOLD
— or use this coupon to order directly from the publisher.

NGAIO MARSH

MORE BEST SELLING PAPERBACKS BY ONE OF YOUR FAVORITE AUTHORS...

	V3613	BLACK AS HE'S PAINTED $1.25
	A4391	DEATH IN A WHITE TIE $1.50
	V3184	DEATH OF A FOOL $1.25
	V3158	HAND IN GLOVE $1.25
	V2986	A MAN LAY DEAD $1.25
	V3321	NIGHT AT THE VULCAN $1.25
	V2994	THE NURSING HOME MURDER $1.25
	A3353	OVERTURE TO DEATH $1.50
	V3384	SINGING IN THE SHROUDS $1.25
	A3081	TIED UP IN TINSEL $1.50
	V3017	VINTAGE MURDER $1.25

Send To: JOVE PUBLICATIONS, INC.
Harcourt Brace Jovanovich, Inc.
Dept. M.O., 757 Third Avenue, New York, N.Y. 10017

NAME

ADDRESS

CITY

STATE   ZIP

I enclose $_____, which includes the total price of all books ordered plus 50¢ per book postage and handling for the first book and 25¢ for each additional. If my total order is $10.00 or more, I understand that Jove Publications, Inc. will pay all postage and handling.

No COD's or stamps. Please allow three to four weeks for delivery. Prices subject to change.

NT-20

Are you missing out on some great Jove/HBJ books?

"You can have any title in print at Jove/HBJ delivered right to your door! To receive your Jove/HBJ Shop-At-Home Catalog, send us 25¢ together with the label below showing your name and address.

JOVE PUBLICATIONS, INC.
Harcourt Brace Jovanovich, Inc.
Dept. M.O., 757 Third Avenue, New York, N.Y. 10017

NAME_____

ADDRESS_____

CITY_____STATE_____

NT-1   ZIP_____